CRESSIDA BLYTHEWOOD

The Duke's Scandalous Proposal

First edition

This book was professionally typeset on Reedsy.
Find out more at reedsy.com

Contents

1

Prolog

I woke up feeling short of breath, my chest rising and falling too quickly for the serene morning that should have greeted me. The air was warmer than it ought to be, almost stifling, despite the chill of the season. I should have felt cold, lying under silk sheets that weren't mine, but instead, I was wrapped in an unfamiliar heat that made my skin prickle.

I tried to drift back to sleep, convincing myself that this was just another restless night. But then, the realization struck me like a bucket of icy water. The usually soft feather pillow beneath my head felt oddly firm. And then— heaven help me—it moved.

The pillow turned its back on me.

I nearly screamed. I bit my lip, tasting copper, and prayed fervently that this was just a bizarre dream—a feverish, wine-induced hallucination from last night's ball. But no, reality crashed over me when the pillow-turned-man murmured in his sleep, a deep rumble that sent a shockwave straight through me.

My eyes snapped open, and I stared at the ceiling, heart pounding. It wasn't the grand chandelier of my family's manor that greeted me, nor the soft pink canopy of my own bed. This was a different room altogether—rich, opulent, and distinctly masculine. The walls were lined with dark wood panels, heavy velvet curtains blocking out the morning sun. A fire crackled in the hearth, the only light in the otherwise shadowed room. This was no place I recognized, no safe haven of mine. If I'm not in my room, then where am I?

My heart hammered in my chest as I turned my head to confirm what my body already knew: I wasn't alone.

Beside me, nestled in the sheets, was a man. Not just any man, but a man who was very much *not* dressed. His broad back was turned toward me, muscles rippling under bronzed skin that seemed to glow in the firelight. His jet-black hair was tousled, as though he had been tossing and turning all night.

My blood ran cold.

Slowly, carefully, I lifted the edge of the blanket, praying to find the safety of my nightdress still clinging to my body. But my prayers went unanswered. I was as bare as the day I was born. And both of us stark naked, our clothes strewn about like casualties of some nocturnal skirmish.

"Oh, my God. Oh, my God. Oh, my God," I whispered frantically, the words tumbling from my lips in a breathless chant.

I bolted upright, clutching the blanket to my chest as if it could somehow shield me from the reality of what had happened. I scanned the room for my clothes, panic rising with every passing second. My gown from last night was strewn across the floor, the delicate fabric crumpled and discarded. My undergarments were nowhere to be seen.

I scrambled out of the bed, my legs trembling as I stood, desperately trying to gather the remnants of my dignity along with my clothes. I didn't dare look back at the man—the stranger—who had shared my bed. But I couldn't stop myself from stealing one last glance before I fled.

All I saw was his back, strong and broad, and the dark tumble of hair against the pillow. I didn't know who he was, but that didn't matter. What mattered was that I, Adelaide Blair, daughter of an Earl, had just woken up naked in a bed that wasn't mine, beside a man who wasn't supposed to be there. And in the process, I had lost something I could never get back.

Cursing under my breath, I yanked on my gown, not caring about the rumples or the missing stays. My hands shook as I fumbled with the door handle, throwing one last glance at the room that would forever haunt me.

Then I ran—ran from the room, from the man, from the truth that now clung to me like a scarlet letter. Because besides waking up naked next to a stranger, I had woken up this morning having lost my virginity.

And I hadn't the faintest idea who had taken it.

2

A Night to Forget

I don't think I've ever moved so quickly in my life. My heart pounded in my chest as I darted through the narrow alleys behind the manor, the hem of my gown clutched tightly in one hand to keep it from dragging in the dirt. The sun was barely rising, and the streets were mercifully empty—no witnesses to my disgrace. I kept my head down, praying no one would recognize me if they happened to glance out of a window.

The back door to our family's manor loomed ahead, a small, unassuming entrance that led straight into the kitchens. I tapped on it with trembling fingers, and a moment later, it creaked open to reveal Betsy, our maid, who took one look at me and gasped.

"Miss Adelaide! What on earth—"

"Shh!" I hissed, glancing over my shoulder as if the very walls had ears. "Betsy, please. I need your help."

Her eyes widened, but to her credit, she didn't ask any questions. Instead, she ushered me inside, herding me quickly up the back stairs to my bedchamber. We moved in silence, the only sound the soft swish of my skirts and the rapid thud of my heart. Once we were safely behind the door, I sagged against it, closing my eyes and exhaling a long, shaky breath.

"Miss Adelaide," Betsy began cautiously, "what happened? You look like you've seen a ghost."

I let out a short, humorless laugh. "Worse than a ghost, Betsy. Much worse."

She frowned, her brow furrowed with concern. "Are you hurt?"

"No," I said quickly, though in truth, I wasn't entirely sure. I felt... different. Raw. "Just... terribly confused. And possibly ruined."

Betsy's mouth dropped open, but before she could launch into a tirade of questions, I pushed myself away from the door and staggered toward the washstand. "I need a bath," I muttered, barely able to meet my own eyes in the mirror as I began unfastening my dress. "And perhaps a scalding."

Without a word, Betsy moved to fetch the bathwater, leaving me alone with my reflection. The girl staring back at me was pale, her hair wild and her eyes wide with the kind of fear that one experiences only in nightmares. I looked every bit the part of a woman who had woken up in a strange bed beside a strange man, and there was no hiding it.

What have I done?

The thought echoed through my mind as I slipped out of my gown and stepped into the steaming bath Betsy had prepared. The hot water was a welcome relief, but it did nothing to ease the tight knot of anxiety in my chest.

I closed my eyes, sinking into the water, and tried to piece together the fragments of the previous night. It had all started with that damned invitation...

The coveted invitation had arrived a week ago, a delicate piece of parchment adorned with the crest of the Imperial Family. It was the event of the season—a grand ball celebrating the founding of the kingdom, and every eligible young lady within a hundred miles was desperate to attend.

My mother had been beside herself with excitement, insisting that this would be *the* night for me to finally catch the eye of Colin, my oldest, dearest friend. Well, perhaps not so much "dearest" as "unwitting object of my unrequited affections," but that was neither here nor there. This ball, my mother declared, would be the moment Colin saw me as more than just the girl who used to chase frogs with him in the garden.

The preparations had been endless—choosing the perfect gown, coaxing my hair into an elegant arrangement, listening to my sister Evelyn's advice on how to "subtly" capture Colin's attention. By the time the evening of the ball arrived, I was a bundle of nerves, my emotions swinging wildly between hope and sheer terror.

As soon as we stepped into the grand hall of the palace, I was overwhelmed by the splendor of it all. The room was filled with nobility, the air thick with the scent of roses and expensive perfume. Chandeliers sparkled overhead, casting a golden glow over the glittering throng. And there, across the room, was Colin—tall, handsome, and utterly oblivious to the chaos raging in my heart.

I spent the first hour trying to work up the courage to approach him, cursing the fluttering in my stomach every time our eyes met. When he finally crossed the room to ask me to dance, I thought my heart might burst right then and there.

He was charming, as always, his smile warm and familiar. For a brief moment, as we twirled across the dance floor, it felt as though all the years of friendship might finally blossom into something more. But even as I clung to that hope, I couldn't shake the nagging feeling that something was off. Colin was distracted, his gaze flickering over my shoulder as though searching for someone else.

Still, I chose to ignore it, determined to make the most of our dance. After all, hadn't I waited long enough for this moment? But as the music ended and Colin excused himself, I saw it—the subtle shift in his expression, the way his eyes lit up as they caught sight of someone behind me.

Curious and more than a little desperate, I followed him out onto the veranda, hoping for... well, I don't know what I was hoping for. Perhaps just a private word, or even a simple smile. But what I found was something that shattered my heart into a thousand pieces.

Colin, my dear, oblivious Colin, was standing there in the moonlight, his arms wrapped around another woman. They were so caught up in each other that they didn't even notice me standing there, watching as he pressed a tender kiss to her lips.

The rest of the evening passed in a blur of heartbreak and humiliation. I barely remember fleeing the veranda, though I must have, because the next thing I knew, I was back inside, desperately trying to hold myself together in the midst of the glittering crowd. The pain was overwhelming, a sharp, searing ache that no amount of bravado could mask.

And so, in a moment of sheer madness, I turned to the one thing I had never before considered—alcohol.

The water had gone tepid by the time Betsy returned to pull me from my reverie. "Miss Adelaide," she said gently, holding out a towel, "you should get out before you catch cold."

I nodded, reluctantly leaving the comfort of the bath and wrapping the towel around myself. As I stood there, dripping and lost in thought, the events of the previous night replayed in my mind like a cruel joke.

The dancing, the veranda, the kiss... and then the wine. Too much wine. I remember slipping away from the ball, my head spinning, my heart aching. I remember wandering through the gardens, the cool night air doing nothing to calm my frayed nerves.

And then...

Nothing.

Nothing until I woke up this morning in that unfamiliar bed.

I shivered, pulling the towel tighter around me as the implications of what had happened settled heavily on my shoulders. My reputation was in tatters, and worse—I had lost something that could never be recovered.

But who was he? The man with the jet-black hair and the broad back? I had no idea, and the thought of facing him, of ever seeing him again, made me feel sick.

"Betsy," I whispered, my voice trembling, "please don't tell anyone about this. Not a soul."

"Of course not, Miss," she replied, her expression full of sympathy. "I won't breathe a word. But... what will you do?"

I stared at my reflection, seeing a different woman than the one who had left for the ball last night. "I don't know," I admitted. "But whatever happens next, I'll have to face it."

3

Reflections of a Ruined Woman

Alone in my room, I finally let out the breath I'd been holding since I stepped through the back door of the manor. The bath had washed away the grime of the night, but not the gnawing anxiety that now clawed at my insides. I stood in front of my mirror, my reflection staring back at me with wide, haunted eyes. My hair was still damp, my skin flushed from the heat of the bath, but I hardly recognized the woman who gazed back at me.

What have you done, Adelaide?

I reached out and touched the cool glass, as if I could somehow wipe away the shame that clung to me like a second skin. But the fear, the self-recrimination, they were all too real. What if that man—whoever he was—decided to make our encounter public? My reputation would be in ruins, and I would be the subject of every whispered conversation, every cruel jest. I'd be labeled a wanton, a fallen woman, and there would be no recovering from that.

And if he were a madman? My stomach churned at the thought. What if he decided to threaten me, to put our scandalous night in the newspaper for all of London to read? Or worse, what if he was a married man who would force me into becoming his mistress, using that night as leverage? The idea of being kept as someone's dirty little secret made my skin crawl.

I shuddered, wrapping my arms around myself as if I could somehow protect what little innocence I had left. My mind raced, conjuring up increasingly horrific scenarios. What if he was a fat, bald widower, an old man who wanted a young wife to warm his bed in his twilight years? The thought was enough to make me gag. No, no, no! I couldn't allow my life to be dictated by a single reckless night.

And then, the most terrifying thought of all crept in, making my heart skip a beat.

What if I'm pregnant?

My hand flew to my stomach, and I stared at my reflection, horrified. This had been my first time—my first and, I'd always imagined, my last until I was safely wed. What if the consequences of that night would show themselves in a few months, with no wedding ring to legitimize it? I would be shunned, cast out from society, forced to live in seclusion with a child born out of wedlock.

No, no, no! I refused to let that happen.

There was only one solution. I had to find a husband—quickly. Someone respectable, someone who could offer me the protection of his name before any scandal had the chance to take root. I had always resisted my mother's attempts to parade me in front of eligible bachelors, secretly clinging to the hope that Colin would one day propose. But Colin was a fantasy, a dream that had shattered on the veranda last night. He was lost to me, and my heartache over him paled in comparison to the terror of what might happen if I didn't act swiftly.

And yet, Colin wasn't the first man I'd fallen for with such misguided hope. Oh no, I had a history of romantic misjudgments that stretched back to my very first season. There had been Lord Alaric, the handsome viscount who had charmed me with his poetry and kind eyes, only for me to discover he was far more interested in my dowry than in my heart. Then there was Sir Geoffrey, the dashing war hero who had swept me off my feet—until I learned he was already secretly engaged to a lady in London. And let's not forget Mr. Elliott, the charming rake who made me laugh like no one else but left me heartbroken when he ran off with my best friend's cousin.

Why had I always been so prone to falling for the wrong man? Perhaps it was my tendency to see only the best in people, to believe in the fairy tale of true love despite all evidence to the contrary. Or perhaps it was simply bad luck—though I had long ago stopped believing that fate had much to do with my romantic misfortunes. Whatever the reason, it had left me with a string of disappointments and a heart that was far too easily bruised.

I closed my eyes and took a deep breath, trying to steady my nerves. The image of Colin kissing that woman flashed through my mind, sharp and clear as if it had happened just moments ago. His hands on her waist, his lips on hers, the way they had looked at each other with such tenderness. It was as though they were the only two people in the world, and the realization hit me like a punch to the gut.

Why had I wasted so much time on a man who clearly never saw me the way I saw him? It was a cruel twist of fate that just as I was ready to let him go, I found myself facing a problem far more pressing than a broken heart.

I needed a husband, and I needed one now. Someone reliable, someone who wouldn't leave me stranded on the precipice of scandal. But how could I trust myself to make the right choice when my heart had always led me astray? I would have to be practical, to put aside my foolish dreams of love and passion and focus on what truly mattered: security, stability, and above all, the preservation of my reputation.

Because this time, the stakes were far too high to indulge in another mistake.

My sister Anne had always been more than eager to attend social gatherings and meet potential suitors, something I had always avoided with a quiet disdain. How foolish I had been, thinking I could afford to wait for Colin to come to his senses. No more. If anyone asked me to attend a dinner party, a ball, even a picnic, I would say yes without hesitation. I would parade myself in front of every eligible man in London if that's what it took.

"Adelaide," I whispered to my reflection, "you're going to marry the first respectable man who asks you. And you're going to do it before anyone finds out what happened last night."

It was a simple plan, but it was all I had. I straightened my shoulders, trying to ignore the dread that still lurked in the pit of my stomach. There was no time to waste on regrets or fears. I would go with Anne to every social event, smile at every eligible bachelor, and accept the first proposal that came my way. I would be a dutiful wife, respectable, proper, and if I was lucky, I might even find a man I could tolerate for the rest of my life.

As for love... I had been foolish to believe in it. Love was a luxury I could no longer afford. Not when my reputation, my future, and possibly even my life were at stake.

I sighed, feeling a pang of loss for the girl I had been just yesterday— innocent, hopeful, and hopelessly naive. She was gone now, replaced by a woman who had seen too much and who knew that the world was not as kind as she had once believed.

"Goodbye, Colin," I murmured, my voice barely above a whisper. "Goodbye to all those foolish dreams."

Because from this day forward, I would live in reality, and reality was a place where women like me didn't have the luxury of waiting for love. We had to seize what we could, protect what was ours, and pray that fate would be kinder than it had been so far.

With one last glance at my reflection, I turned away from the mirror and squared my shoulders. It was time to face the world with a new purpose.

Find a husband. Save your reputation. Forget last night.

Simple enough. Now all I had to do was pretend I believed it.

4

The Lady's Reckoning

I woke up alone.

The bed beside me was cold, the sheets twisted and abandoned, much like my own peace of mind. I stretched, feeling the tightness in my muscles, and then sat up, rubbing a hand over my face. My head throbbed—not from drink, as I hadn't indulged nearly as much as I could have last night—but from the absurdity of the situation.

The morning light filtered through the heavy curtains, casting the room in a muted, golden glow. It was a beautiful day to be waking up in a royal guest chamber, a room reserved for the kingdom's most esteemed visitors. Yet, the bed was far too large for just one occupant. And this morning, it was only I who remained, while the other half of the story had fled into the shadows.

I scratched my head, my fingers brushing over the short strands of hair still damp from last night's unplanned dip. That woman... Adelaide Blair... She was gone, but her presence lingered in every wrinkle of the sheets, every misplaced pillow.

Adelaide. I remembered everything.

The ball, the fountains, the complete and utter chaos of the night. It played back in my mind like a poorly staged farce, except there was no audience laughing in the wings. Just me, sitting here alone, wondering how in the devil it had all happened.

I had seen her first when she was standing at the edge of the fountain, her beautiful gown glistening under the moonlight, her balance more than a little questionable. Adelaide Blair, the Earl's second daughter—known for her wit, her lively spirit, and apparently, her absolute lack of control when she'd had too much to drink.

She had been swaying precariously, and though I had no particular fondness for playing the hero, it was clear she was about to take a plunge. Naturally, I'd gone to help her, thinking that perhaps I could guide her back to solid ground without too much fuss. But before I could say a word, she'd turned those bright, hazel eyes on me, brimming with an emotion I couldn't quite place.

"You!" she had slurred, grabbing my collar with surprising strength. "You hurt me!"

That was news to me. I hadn't even known she knew my name, let alone that I had somehow wronged her. I had tried to explain, but she wouldn't hear it. Before I could utter a single word, she had kissed me.

I still felt the ghost of that kiss—unexpected, warm, and entirely disorienting. I hadn't returned it, of course. Not because I wasn't tempted, but because it had come so completely out of nowhere. I'd tried to push her away, to put some distance between us before the situation could spiral any further out of control.

But then, in the midst of that hurried attempt to extricate myself, she'd slipped. And naturally, I, with all the grace of a newborn foal, had gone down with her.

The pool had been cold—shockingly so—and I still remembered the way the water had drenched us both, ruining her gown and my dignity in one fell swoop. The fountain had splashed around us as if mocking the scene, and there we were, two soaked fools in the middle of it all.

And then, she kissed me again.

This time, I hadn't been able to push her away. This time, I hadn't *wanted* to push her away.

There, in the middle of that ridiculous fountain, I'd felt something—something I hadn't felt before. Something that kept me rooted to the spot, drowning in more than just the water that soaked our clothes. And though I knew I should have stopped it, known that this was a recipe for scandal, I had been frozen. No, not frozen—enchanted. Ensnared by the feel of her lips on mine, by the madness of it all.

But reason had reasserted itself. Not wanting to add any further spectacle to the night, I had taken Adelaide to the guest chambers, summoned a servant for fresh clothes, and planned to leave her to sleep it off in peace.

Except she hadn't been interested in peace.

She'd pushed me onto the bed—*pushed* me!—and before I knew it, her lips were on mine again, with a fervor that made my head spin. She had mumbled something about needing to erase the marks her kisses had left on my lips, and I, in my state of damp bewilderment, hadn't quite managed to protest.

And then... well, then it had all happened.

I sighed, squeezing the pendant of her necklace that she had left behind—an item that had slipped off in the fray and remained as a reminder of the night I had never expected to have. A night that had begun with an innocent, if slightly tipsy, encounter by a fountain and ended with my entire world turned on its head.

Damn it all. She had taken more than my first kiss; she had taken my virginity. And she had the audacity to flee without so much as a goodbye?

I stood up, dropping the necklace onto the bedside table and running a hand through my hair again, trying to collect my thoughts. The warmth of the morning sun did nothing to soothe the growing tension in my chest. I wasn't just angry—I was determined.

She couldn't just run away from this, from me. Whether she remembered it or not, she would be held accountable. I wasn't some scoundrel who flitted from woman to woman without care. I was Duke Bastian Lightwood, a man of principle, a man of honor—at least, I had been until last night.

Well, if she thought she could escape so easily, she was sorely mistaken. I would see her again, and she would answer for what she had done.

No more running, no more hiding. This wasn't over. Not by a long shot.

5

Life as Usual?

The morning sun streamed through the lace curtains of my bedroom, casting delicate patterns across the wooden floor. Birds chirped merrily outside, their songs a cruel reminder that life continued unabated, indifferent to the turmoil churning within me. I sat at my vanity, brush in hand, attempting to tame the unruly curls that seemed to mirror my chaotic thoughts.

"Adelaide, are you ready?" My sister Anne's voice floated through the closed door, laced with impatience. "We're going to be late for our ride!"

"Just a moment!" I called back, forcing a brightness into my tone that I didn't feel. I took a deep breath, setting the brush down and surveying my reflection. My cheeks held a natural flush, a testament to the restless night I'd endured, and my eyes bore the faint shadows of sleeplessness. Yet, I managed a smile, small and fragile, before standing and smoothing the skirts of my riding habit.

Today would be ordinary. Today, I would reclaim my routine, burying the memory of that night beneath layers of normalcy. I opened the door to find Anne leaning against the opposite wall, her arms crossed and a teasing smirk on her lips.

"Finally," she said, rolling her eyes. "I was beginning to think you'd fallen back asleep."

"Perish the thought," I replied, linking my arm through hers. "I wouldn't miss our ride for the world."

Together, we descended the grand staircase, the familiar scent of lavender polish and fresh flowers enveloping us. The manor bustled with activity— maids dusting, footmen carrying trays, and Mother's voice drifting from the drawing room as she dictated a letter. It was comforting, this rhythm of daily life, and I clung to it like a lifeline.

Outside, the crisp morning air greeted us, invigorating and fresh. Our horses awaited, their coats gleaming in the sunlight. I approached my mare, Luna, her gentle eyes meeting mine as I stroked her muzzle.

"Ready for an adventure, girl?" I whispered, pressing my forehead against hers. She nickered softly, the sound easing the tightness in my chest.

Anne mounted her stallion with practiced ease, her auburn hair tucked neatly beneath her riding hat. She looked over at me, a glint of mischief in her eyes. "Race you to the oak tree?"

I laughed, the sound surprising me with its genuineness. "You're on."

We set off, the wind whipping past as our horses galloped across the open fields. The world blurred, a canvas of vibrant greens and blues, and for a moment, the weight of my worries lifted. The exhilaration of the ride consumed me, each hoofbeat a drum drowning out the whispers of doubt.

Anne pulled ahead, her laughter carried on the breeze, and I urged Luna faster, the gap between us closing. The ancient oak loomed ahead, its sprawling branches a familiar landmark. At the last moment, Luna surged forward, and we reached the tree in a tie, both breathless and grinning.

"Well," Anne panted, dismounting, "I suppose we'll have to call that a draw."

I slid from Luna's back, patting her neck affectionately. "Agreed. Though I think Luna deserves extra oats for her efforts."

We settled beneath the oak, the shade offering respite from the sun's growing warmth. Anne plucked a blade of grass, twirling it between her fingers as she gazed out over the countryside.

"Did you enjoy the anniversary ball the other night?" she asked casually, though her eyes flicked to me with keen interest.

My heart stuttered, memories threatening to surface. I forced a nonchalant shrug. "It was as expected. Crowded, loud, the usual fanfare."

Anne raised an eyebrow. "Really? I thought perhaps you'd have more to say, given how quickly you disappeared."

Panic flared. Had she noticed my absence? Had others? I kept my expression neutral, schooling my features into a mask of indifference. "I wasn't feeling well. Too much excitement, I suppose."

"Hmm," she mused, her gaze piercing. "Well, you missed quite the spectacle. Apparently, Lady Beaumont fainted after Lord Montgomery proposed to her."

I seized the change in topic with relief. "Did she accept before or after swooning?"

Anne laughed, the sound light and infectious. "After, of course. It wouldn't be proper otherwise."

We shared a smile, the moment easing the tension that had coiled within me. Yet, beneath the surface, unease simmered. How many had noticed my absence? Had whispers already begun to spread? I pushed the thoughts aside, determined not to let them ruin this fleeting peace.

After our ride, I retreated to the solarium, a sanctuary of sunlight and serenity. My easel stood by the window, a canvas awaiting inspiration. I gathered my paints, the familiar scent of linseed oil and pigments wrapping around me like a comforting embrace.

As I dipped my brush into vibrant blues and soft greens, I let my mind drift, strokes flowing with practiced ease. Painting had always been my escape, a realm where colors spoke louder than words, where emotions could be translated into shades and textures.

Hours passed unnoticed, the canvas blossoming into a serene landscape—a meadow bathed in twilight, stars beginning to wink into existence. It was peaceful, a stark contrast to the turmoil within me. I stepped back, assessing my work, and for a moment, contentment settled.

"Adelaide," Mother's voice cut through the quiet, startling me. I turned to find her standing in the doorway, her expression a mix of affection and purpose. "There you are. I've been looking for you."

"Is everything alright?" I asked, setting my palette aside.

"Quite. I wanted to inform you that we've been invited to the Fitzwilliam's soirée this evening. A small gathering, nothing too grand."

A knot formed in my stomach. Another social event, another opportunity for scrutiny. Yet, I knew refusal wasn't an option. If I were to find a husband, as I'd resolved, I couldn't shy away from such occasions.

"Of course," I replied, forcing a smile. "I'll prepare accordingly."

Mother beamed, crossing the room to squeeze my hand. "Wonderful. Wear the lavender gown; it brings out your eyes."

With that, she departed, leaving me alone once more. I stared at the half-finished painting, the tranquility it depicted now feeling distant. The prospect of the soirée loomed, a reminder that despite my attempts to resume life as usual, the specter of that night remained.

As dusk approached, I found myself seated at my vanity again, Anne assisting with the intricate braiding of my hair. The lavender gown hugged my form, the silk cool against my skin. I met my own gaze in the mirror, searching for signs of the woman I'd been before—innocent, unburdened.

"Adelaide," Anne's voice was soft, a rare seriousness coloring her tone. "Are you alright? You've seemed... distracted lately."

I hesitated, the urge to confide in her battling with the fear of exposure. Anne was my sister, my confidante, yet some secrets were too perilous to share.

"I'm fine," I lied, offering a reassuring smile. "Just preoccupied with my painting."

She studied me, skepticism evident, but chose not to press further. "Well, if anyone can charm the ton, it's you."

I laughed lightly. "Flattery will get you everywhere."

As we descended the staircase, the murmur of voices drifted from the foyer. Father stood by the door, adjusting his cuffs, while Mother fussed over his cravat. They looked up as we approached, pride shining in their eyes.

"My beautiful daughters," Father proclaimed, extending an arm to each of us. "Shall we?"

The carriage ride was filled with polite chatter, the kind that skimmed the surface without delving into depth. I participated, laughing at Anne's quips, responding to Mother's reminders of decorum. Yet, beneath it all, a current of anxiety thrummed.

The Fitzwilliam estate was aglow, lanterns casting a warm luminescence over the manicured gardens. As we entered the grand hall, the familiar cacophony of laughter, clinking glasses, and orchestral melodies enveloped us. I plastered on a smile, determined to play my part.

Throughout the evening, I danced, conversed, and laughed at the appropriate moments. Suitors approached, some bold, others tentative, and I engaged them all with practiced grace. There was Lord Everett, who bowed so low his powdered wig nearly tumbled off; his flattery was excessive, his eyes too keen, and I found his company tiresome. Then there was Sir William, a quiet, bookish man who spoke earnestly of his love for astronomy. Though I found his passion endearing, I could not summon more than polite interest. And finally, Mr. Clarke, whose dance was so full of blunders that I spent most of the time suppressing giggles rather than engaging in conversation.

Their words washed over me, hollow and insubstantial, failing to stir anything within me but a longing for the evening to end. I smiled where it was expected, laughed when prompted, but my heart remained untouched, my thoughts drifting far from the glittering spectacle around me.

Between dances, I found myself on the terrace, the cool night air a balm against the suffocating atmosphere inside. Stars glittered above, indifferent to the dramas of mortal lives. I leaned against the balustrade, inhaling deeply, seeking solace in the silence of the night. The sky stretched endlessly above, a vast expanse of darkness speckled with light, and for a moment, I allowed myself to simply breathe, to exist without the weight of expectations pressing down on me.

"Escaping the throng?" a voice drawled beside me.

I turned, startled, to find Lord Henry Sinclair, a notorious rake with a reputation as dark as his ebony hair. His piercing blue eyes regarded me with a mixture of amusement and something else—something that set my nerves on edge.

"Simply seeking fresh air," I replied, maintaining a polite distance.

He smirked, stepping closer. "I can't blame you. These gatherings can be dreadfully dull."

I offered a noncommittal smile, wishing for an excuse to depart. His proximity was unsettling, his gaze too knowing.

"Miss Blair," he began, his voice low, "I couldn't help but notice your absence during the latter part of the kingdom's anniversary celebration."

My heart raced, fear lancing through me. "I wasn't feeling well."

"Ah," he murmured, his lips curling. "Understandable. Such events can be... overwhelming."

I swallowed, the implication in his tone unmistakable. Did he know? Had he seen something? Panic threatened to consume me, but I maintained my composure.

"Indeed," I replied coolly. "If you'll excuse me, Lord Sinclair, I believe my next dance is about to begin."

He inclined his head, a glint in his eyes. "Of course. Until next time, Miss Blair."

I fled, heart pounding, the walls seeming to close in around me. The remainder of the soirée passed in a haze, my smiles forced, my laughter brittle. But as I stepped back into the grand hall, a strange sensation washed over me. It started as a prickling at the back of my neck, like the lightest touch of a feather, and then it grew—an inexplicable feeling that someone was watching me. I tried to dismiss it as nerves, but the sensation only intensified, settling in my chest like a stone.

The ballroom was alive with the usual sights and sounds—ladies and gentlemen whirling across the dance floor, the soft clinking of glasses, the orchestra playing a lively waltz—but I couldn't shake the feeling that someone's eyes were fixed on me, observing my every move.

I resisted the urge to turn around, unwilling to reveal my discomfort. Instead, I forced a smile and moved through the room with practiced grace, greeting acquaintances and exchanging pleasantries. Yet, beneath the surface, my heart raced, my senses on high alert.

As I neared the edge of the dance floor, I hesitated, scanning the crowd discreetly. Was it Lord Sinclair watching me, his piercing blue eyes tracking my every step? Or was it someone else entirely? The thought sent a shiver down my spine. In a room full of people, how could I possibly identify the source of my unease?

"Adelaide!" Anne's voice called to me, breaking through my thoughts. I turned to find her approaching with Mr. Hammond, his cheerful smile as bright as ever.

"Anne," I replied, hoping my voice sounded steadier than I felt. "How lovely to see you enjoying yourself."

"You must come join us. Mr. Hammond has just suggested the most delightful idea for a picnic next week," Anne said, her excitement evident.

Mr. Hammond bowed. "Miss Blair, it would be my honor if you and your family would attend. The gardens at my estate are particularly beautiful this time of year."

I forced a polite smile, my mind still half-focused on the unnerving sensation that had followed me inside. "That sounds wonderful, Mr. Hammond. I'm sure it would be a lovely outing."

Anne continued to chatter with Mr. Hammond, but I found myself only half-listening. My gaze drifted across the room, searching for anything out of place, anyone who might be the source of the watchful eyes I felt on me. But the ballroom seemed perfectly ordinary, filled with the familiar faces of the ton.

Excusing myself from Anne and Mr. Hammond's company, I made my way to the refreshment table, hoping a glass of lemonade might calm my nerves. As I sipped the cool drink, I couldn't shake the feeling that I was being observed, studied even, and it was all I could do to keep my composure.

Then, out of the corner of my eye, I caught a flicker of movement. I turned my head sharply, but whoever had been there vanished before I could see them clearly. All that remained was the faint sway of the curtains by the far window, as if someone had just slipped behind them.

My heart pounded as I approached the window, each step measured and deliberate. The music from the ballroom masked any sounds, but I strained to hear, hoping to catch some sign of the mysterious observer. When I reached the window, I hesitated, my hand hovering just above the curtain. Every instinct told me to walk away, to leave this strange game of cat and mouse behind. But curiosity—and fear—compelled me to push the curtain aside.

The space behind was empty, the window slightly ajar to let in the cool night air. A gust of wind caught the fabric of the drapes, making them billow gently. There was no one there.

I let out a shaky breath, my fingers tightening around the curtain. Had I imagined it? Or had someone really been there, watching me? And if so, who were they?

A chill crept up my spine as a thought struck me. What if the person watching me tonight was connected to that night? Was it possible that the stranger whose bed I'd woken up in—the dark-haired man whose back was the only part of him I had seen—was now stalking me? The idea was terrifying, and yet, it made a disturbing sort of sense. What if he hadn't forgotten about that night, as I had desperately hoped? What if he had been searching for me, and tonight, he had found me?

I stepped back from the window, letting the curtain fall back into place. The sense of being watched had faded, but the unease lingered, gnawing at the edges of my thoughts. Whoever had been watching me was gone, but I couldn't shake the feeling that this wasn't the end. Whoever it was—whether the stranger from that night or someone else—they weren't finished with me yet.

I forced myself to return to the party, though every instinct screamed at me to flee. The rest of the evening passed in a blur of forced smiles and hollow conversation. Lord Everett, with his excessive flattery, tried in vain to capture my attention, but I found his company exhausting. Sir William spoke earnestly of his love for astronomy, but my mind was elsewhere, and Mr. Clarke's blundering dance was more amusing than anything else. None of them sparked even the faintest flicker of interest.

As the hour grew late, I finally excused myself, pleading fatigue. My family was quick to follow suit, and soon we were bundled into the carriage, the night's events replaying in my mind like a puzzle missing crucial pieces.

When we arrived home, I climbed the stairs to my room, the sense of unease still clinging to me like a shadow. I closed the door behind me, leaning against it for support as I tried to process everything that had happened. Was the man from that night now stalking me? Was he watching me from the shadows, waiting for the right moment to reveal himself? The thought sent a fresh wave of fear through me.

As I prepared for bed, I couldn't stop thinking about the stranger whose back I had only glimpsed in the morning light. Who was he? And why had he come into my life, only to haunt me now? The more I thought about it, the more I realized that I had no choice. I would have to confront whatever was coming, whether it was the dark-haired stranger or someone else entirely.

6

Unseen and Unforgiven

The ballroom was alive with the usual sights and sounds—ladies and gentlemen whirling across the dance floor, the soft clinking of glasses, the orchestra playing a lively waltz—but all of it faded into the background for me. My attention was fixed on one person, and one person only: Adelaide Blair.

It had been weeks since that fateful night, yet every time I closed my eyes, I was transported back to that moment. Her warmth, her touch, the way her body had responded to mine—it was a memory that haunted me, driving me mad with a desire I could not shake. But what infuriated me the most was that while I lay awake night after night, tormented by the memory of her, she seemed completely unaffected. She moved through the room with a serene smile, her laugh light and carefree as she engaged in conversation after conversation with other men, as if our night together had never happened.

My jaw clenched as I watched her from the shadows of the ballroom. How could she be so unburdened, so at ease, when I was consumed by thoughts of her? Didn't she remember? Didn't she care? The way she spoke to Mr. Hammond, her eyes sparkling as she entertained his talk of a picnic—was it possible that she had forgotten everything? Or worse, was she deliberately pretending that nothing had happened between us?

As I watched Adelaide, a wave of irritation coursed through me. I had expected something different after that night, some acknowledgment of what we had shared. But instead, she acted as if it had been nothing more than a fleeting moment, easily discarded and forgotten. It was infuriating. Why should I be the one to suffer while she went about her life as if nothing had changed?

I had to know if she was truly as unaffected as she appeared, or if this was all a charade. That's why I was here tonight, lurking in the shadows, my gaze never straying far from her. I needed to see if there was any flicker of recognition in her eyes, any hint that she was as tormented by our night together as I was.

But there was nothing. As she moved gracefully across the dance floor, exchanging pleasantries with the other guests, there wasn't a single sign that she was anything other than completely at ease. Meanwhile, I was a wreck—a ball of frustration and pent-up desire, unable to focus on anything other than the way her lips had felt against mine, the way her body had fit perfectly in my arms.

As I leaned against the column, my fingers tightening around the glass of brandy in my hand, I felt the urge to confront her, to demand answers. How could she be so composed when I was unraveling? But I held back, knowing that an outburst would do nothing to solve the turmoil raging inside me. No, I needed to be patient, to wait for the right moment.

My eyes narrowed as I watched her excusing herself from Mr. Hammond and heading toward the refreshment table. Her smile never faltered, her movements as fluid and graceful as ever. It was maddening. How was she able to carry on like this, as if our night together had meant nothing?

I couldn't take it anymore. I had to know what was going on in that head of hers. Was she deliberately tormenting me, or was she truly as unbothered as she appeared?

When she approached the window, a flicker of movement caught my eye. She was looking for something—or someone. My heart pounded in my chest as she reached for the curtain, her hand hesitating before she pushed it aside. I tensed, expecting to be caught, but when she stepped back, her expression was one of confusion and frustration. She hadn't found what she was looking for.

I released a breath I hadn't realized I was holding, a twisted sense of satisfaction curling in my chest. Perhaps she wasn't as unaffected as she appeared. Perhaps she did remember that night, after all.

As the evening wore on, I continued to watch her, my frustration only growing as she engaged with one man after another. Lord Everett, Sir William, Mr. Clarke—each one tried to capture her attention, to win her favor, and she responded to all of them with the same charming smile, the same light laugh. It made my blood boil.

Didn't she realize what she had done to me? How she had consumed my thoughts, my every waking moment? Why did I have to suffer alone while she was free to flirt and dance as if nothing had happened?

I had half a mind to march over there and drag her away from the crowd, to force her to acknowledge what we had shared. But I knew that wouldn't end well. I couldn't reveal myself—not yet. I needed to be sure, to understand what was going on in her mind before I made my move.

As the night drew to a close and the guests began to leave, I watched Adelaide say her goodbyes, her smile still firmly in place. My fists clenched at my sides. How could she be so calm, so composed, when I was on the verge of losing my mind?

I followed her at a distance as she left the ballroom and made her way to the carriage with her family. My heart pounded in my chest as I watched her ascend the stairs to her room, my mind a whirlwind of frustration and desire. I had to know what she was thinking, why she was able to move on so easily while I was trapped in the memory of that night.

As the carriage pulled away, and I was left alone in the shadows, a thought struck me—a thought that both thrilled and terrified me. What if she wasn't pretending? What if she truly had forgotten? The idea sent a chill down my spine. If that were the case, then I had a decision to make: confront her and force her to remember, or let her go and continue to suffer in silence.

But I couldn't let her go. Not yet. Not when every fiber of my being was still bound to that night, to the memory of her in my arms.

I would find out the truth, one way or another. And when I did, Adelaide would have to face the consequences of what she had done to me. Whether she liked it or not, she would remember that night, and she would know that I hadn't forgotten.

7

The Shocking Proposal

T he morning light filtered through the curtains, casting a warm glow over the breakfast table where my family gathered. The soft clatter of china and the murmurs of conversation filled the room, a peaceful start to the day. But beneath the surface, my thoughts were anything but calm. The events of the previous night at the Fitzwilliam soirée weighed heavily on my mind—the unnerving sensation of being watched, the questions swirling about the identity of the man from that fateful night, and the fear that my secret was teetering on the edge of exposure.

I forced myself to focus on the breakfast before me, though my appetite had long since fled. My mother was engaged in lively conversation with Anne about the upcoming picnic at Mr. Hammond's estate, while Father sipped his coffee, content to listen. It was all so ordinary, so blissfully normal, and yet I felt as if I were standing on the precipice of something terrible.

"Adelaide, darling, you're awfully quiet this morning," my mother observed, her brow furrowing in concern. "Is something the matter?"

I shook my head, offering her a faint smile. "No, Mother, I'm just a bit tired, that's all. The soirée was rather exhausting."

Anne glanced at me, her eyes twinkling with mischief. "Perhaps it was Lord Sinclair's attention that wore you out, Adelaide. He seemed particularly interested in your whereabouts last night."

I stiffened at the mention of his name, the memory of his unsettling gaze sending a chill through me. "Lord Sinclair has a tendency to be overly curious," I replied, keeping my tone light, though my heart pounded in my chest. "I wouldn't read too much into it."

Father chuckled, clearly amused by the exchange. "You ladies do attract quite the attention these days. It's only natural, given your beauty and charm."

I managed a smile, though my thoughts were far from the compliments being thrown my way. What did Lord Sinclair know? Had he seen something that night, or was it just his usual penchant for meddling? And then there was the mysterious figure at the soirée—had that been the same man? My mind raced with possibilities, none of them comforting.

But as I tried to push these thoughts aside, there came an unexpected interruption. A soft knock on the dining room door preceded the entrance of our butler, Mr. Hayes, who carried a silver tray bearing a single, ornate letter. He approached my father with the gravity of one delivering momentous news, and I couldn't help but notice the subtle tension in the air.

"A letter for you, my lord," Mr. Hayes announced, presenting the envelope with a bow.

Father accepted it with a nod, his expression curious as he examined the fine parchment. The crest stamped on the seal caught my eye—a ducal seal, unmistakably grand and formal. My heart skipped a beat, a sense of foreboding settling over me like a heavy cloak.

"A ducal correspondence," Father murmured, breaking the seal with deliberate care. He unfolded the letter, his eyes scanning the page with growing interest. I watched him intently, my stomach knotting as the seconds dragged on. What could it be?

Father cleared his throat, drawing the attention of everyone at the table. "It seems we have received a rather unexpected proposal," he announced, his voice a mixture of pride and astonishment.

"A proposal?" Mother repeated, her eyes widening with excitement. "From whom, darling?"

Father looked up from the letter, his gaze settling on me with an expression I couldn't quite decipher. "From His Grace, the Duke of Lightwood."

The words seemed to echo in the room, bouncing off the walls and reverberating through my very soul. A proposal. From Duke Bastian Lightwood. The man whose reputation as the "Ice Duke" preceded him, a figure both feared and respected throughout society. My heart pounded so loudly I was certain everyone could hear it, my breath catching in my throat as the reality of the situation began to sink in.

The Duke of Lightwood. The man with the jet-black hair and the cold, calculating eyes. The man who had watched me from across the ballroom at other social events but had never spoken a word to me. Could it be...?

"Oh!" Mother gasped, her hands clasping together in delight. "What an extraordinary match! The Duke of Lightwood is one of the most powerful men in the kingdom. This is a tremendous honor!"

Anne's eyes were wide with amazement, and even she seemed momentarily speechless. "A duke, Adelaide. Can you believe it?"

I couldn't. My mind raced with confusion and fear. How could this be happening? Why was the Duke proposing to me, of all people? Could he possibly be the man from that night—the stranger whose bed I had woken up in, the dark-haired man whose back was the only part of him I had seen? The thought sent a shiver through me, a mix of dread and disbelief. Had he somehow found out it was me? And if so, was this proposal his way of holding me accountable, of claiming me for reasons I couldn't fathom?

Father, oblivious to the turmoil raging within me, continued to read the letter aloud. "His Grace writes that he has taken a keen interest in Adelaide and wishes to secure her hand in marriage. He praises her grace and intelligence and believes she would be a worthy Duchess of Lightwood."

A cold sweat broke out along the back of my neck. This wasn't a proposal born of love or even affection; it was a calculated move, a decision made with the same precision the Duke was known for in his business dealings. But why? Why me?

I could hardly breathe, my chest tight with panic. What would happen if I refused? Could I even refuse a duke's proposal? The very thought seemed impossible, unthinkable. My parents would never forgive me, society would never understand. But the idea of marrying a man I barely knew, a man whose reputation was shrouded in mystery and fear.

And yet, what choice did I have? If the Duke was indeed the man from that night, perhaps he had discovered my secret. If he chose to expose what had happened, it would ruin me utterly. My reputation, my family's honor—it would all be destroyed in an instant. But if I accepted...

Mother's voice broke through my thoughts, her tone brimming with excitement. "This is everything we could have dreamed of, Adelaide! A match with the Duke of Lightwood! You'll be a duchess!"

My hands trembled as I gripped the edge of the table, my mind spinning with fear and confusion. This couldn't be happening—it felt like a nightmare from which I couldn't wake. The walls seemed to close in around me, the room growing smaller with every passing second.

"Adelaide, darling, you must be thrilled!" Mother exclaimed, beaming at me with such joy that I could hardly bear it. "This is a dream come true!"

Thrilled? How could I be thrilled when I was teetering on the edge of ruin, when the man I might be forced to marry could very well be the one who haunted my nightmares?

I swallowed hard, forcing myself to speak, though my voice came out barely above a whisper. "I... I'm just... surprised. I had no idea..."

Father's expression softened, his pride evident. "I understand it's a lot to take in, Adelaide. But this is a remarkable opportunity. You will be the Duchess of Lightwood, one of the most esteemed titles in the land. His Grace has made his intentions clear. I expect you to consider this very seriously."

Consider it? How could I not? My thoughts were a chaotic whirl of possibilities and fears. If I accepted, I might save my reputation—but at what cost? A life with a man I feared, a man who might have been the very one to take my innocence that night. Could I ever truly trust him?

And if I refused... No, I couldn't even entertain the thought. Refusal was not an option. My parents were overjoyed at the prospect of such a prestigious match, and the Duke's power was far-reaching. A rejection would bring nothing but disaster.

I nodded slowly, my mind still racing. "Of course, Father. I will... consider it."

"Take your time, dear," Mother said, though her excitement made it clear she expected only one answer. "But I'm sure you'll see that this is the best possible outcome for you."

"Adelaide, you'll be the envy of all the young ladies," Anne squeezed my hand under the table, her eyes sparkling with excitement. "A duchess! Just imagine."

I could imagine all too well—a gilded cage, a life of luxury overshadowed by fear and uncertainty. And yet, what choice did I have? The Duke had presented his proposal to my father, and the expectations were clear. My family would never understand if I hesitated, let alone refused. To reject a Duke was unthinkable, especially one as powerful as Bastian Lightwood.

Had the Duke truly taken an interest in me, or was this proposal a sinister move to trap me in his web of power? I couldn't shake the feeling that something darker lay beneath his seemingly honorable intentions. His eyes had followed me at every social event, always watching, always assessing. And now, without any prior interaction, he had sent a formal proposal to my father. The more I thought about it, the more it felt like a chess move, one designed to corner me, to force my hand.

As the conversation turned to the arrangements and the expected response, I sat in stunned silence, my thoughts consumed by a single question:

What did Duke Bastian Lightwood really want from me?

8

A Dilemma Unfolds

T he moment I could escape the jubilant atmosphere of the dining room, I did. My heart was pounding as I hurried up the grand staircase, my hands trembling as I clutched the banister. The ornate décor of the manor blurred around me, a hazy backdrop to the whirlwind of emotions that had overtaken me.

Duke Bastian Lightwood had proposed. To me.

It felt like a bad dream, one that I couldn't wake from no matter how hard I tried. The truth was, I hadn't the faintest idea what the Duke's intentions were, nor why he had chosen me as the object of his seemingly cold and calculated affection. The very thought of becoming his wife filled me with dread, yet what other choice did I have? To refuse would be unthinkable.

Once inside my chambers, I closed the door behind me and leaned against it, exhaling a long, shaky breath. The familiar surroundings of my room—my bed draped in soft linens, the vanity cluttered with my brushes and perfumes, the painting I had been working on just yesterday—felt strangely distant, as if they belonged to someone else. Someone who wasn't about to be thrust into a life she had never imagined.

I moved to the window, gazing out at the gardens below. The early morning sun bathed the world in a golden light, a stark contrast to the storm raging inside me. What was I to do? My parents' joy at the Duke's proposal was palpable; they saw it as the culmination of all their hopes and dreams for me.

How could I disappoint them? And yet, the idea of marrying a man I barely knew—a man with a reputation as cold as his name—filled me with a fear I could hardly contain.

Who was Duke Bastian Lightwood to me? I had seen him only from a distance, a figure as formidable as his reputation. What could possibly prompt such a sudden proposal? My mind churned with questions, none of them yielding answers.

A soft knock at the door pulled me from my thoughts. "Adelaide?" Anne's voice called out, tentative and gentle.

"Come in," I managed, trying to compose myself as I turned from the window.

Anne slipped into the room, closing the door behind her. Her eyes were wide with curiosity and concern as she approached me. "Are you alright?" she asked, her tone full of sisterly affection. "I can't imagine how overwhelmed you must feel."

I nodded, though words seemed to elude me. "I... I don't know what to think, Anne. This proposal... it's all so sudden, so unexpected."

Anne sat beside me on the edge of the bed, her expression thoughtful. "It is strange, isn't it? I mean, the Duke of Lightwood, of all people! I've never even spoken to him, and I've been to nearly every ball this season. He's so... untouchable."

"I've only ever seen him from a distance," I admitted, twisting my fingers in my lap. "I don't think we've ever exchanged more than a glance, if that. And now he wants to marry me? It makes no sense."

Anne frowned, clearly as puzzled as I was. "It's not as if he's been courting you, either. No one has ever mentioned him being particularly interested in anyone, let alone you. And with his reputation..." She trailed off, a slight shiver running through her. "It just doesn't add up."

I shook my head, trying to make sense of the chaos in my mind. "I can't help but wonder... what is he thinking? Why would he choose me?"

Anne's eyes widened, her curiosity piqued, but she quickly dismissed any serious concern. "Who knows with men like him? He's probably decided that you're the perfect choice for reasons only he understands. Maybe he's just bored with the usual crowd and wants someone who's different."

Her logic was sound, yet the unease remained, gnawing at me like a persistent shadow. I was on the verge of tears, but Anne's presence was a comfort, her familiar scent and gentle touch reminding me that I wasn't alone in this. I could always count on her to lighten the mood, and she didn't disappoint.

After a moment of silence, Anne leaned back, a mischievous glint in her eye. "You know, there must be some reason he's so interested in you, Adelaide. What if he's secretly been watching you for years, smitten by your beauty but too shy to approach?"

I stared at her in disbelief, the absurdity of the notion making me momentarily forget my worries. "Duke Bastian Lightwood? Shy? That's like saying a lion is afraid of its prey!"

Anne grinned, undeterred. "Oh, but wouldn't that be something? The cold and formidable Duke, secretly a hopeless romantic who's been pining for you from afar? Perhaps he's been writing poetry about you in his private chambers, longing for the day he could finally confess his love."

I couldn't help it—I burst out laughing, the tension of the morning finally breaking. The image of the infamous Duke scribbling love sonnets by candlelight was so utterly ridiculous that I could barely breathe from laughing. "Anne, you have the wildest imagination!"

"Well, can you blame me?" she teased, her own laughter bubbling up. "There has to be some explanation, and if it's not that, maybe he's simply enchanted by your kindness and wit. Or perhaps he's a collector of fine art and heard about your painting skills. He could want you to immortalize him on canvas!"

I giggled, the laughter a welcome relief from the burden of my thoughts. "Or perhaps he needs someone to warm his cold, icy heart."

"Exactly!" Anne agreed, her eyes dancing with mischief. "Who better than you, Adelaide? You could be the one to melt the Ice Duke, turn his stone heart into something soft and tender."

We laughed together, the sound echoing through the room, the momentary levity a balm to my frazzled nerves. It felt good to laugh, to imagine a world where the Duke's proposal was nothing more than the result of some whimsical fancy. But as the laughter faded, reality settled back in, heavy and unavoidable.

Anne's smile softened, and she reached out to take my hand. "In all seriousness, Adelaide, I don't know why the Duke proposed, but I do know that you're strong enough to handle whatever comes next. You've always been so brave, even when things seemed impossible."

I squeezed her hand, grateful for her support. "I just wish I knew what I was dealing with. I feel like I'm walking into this blind, with no idea what to expect."

Anne nodded, her expression sympathetic. "It's a lot to take in, I know. But you don't have to make a decision right away. Take some time to think about it, to figure out what you really want. And whatever you decide, I'll be here for you."

Her words were a comfort, but they didn't erase the fear that gnawed at me. I had so many questions, so many doubts, and no clear answers. The Duke's proposal had thrown my world into chaos, and the path ahead was shrouded in uncertainty.

As Anne rose to leave, she gave me one last encouraging smile. "Remember, Adelaide, you're not alone in this. We'll figure it out together."

I nodded, watching as she slipped out of the room, closing the door softly behind her. Alone once more, I returned to the window, gazing out at the gardens below.

The Duke's proposal loomed over me like a dark cloud, and I knew that whatever decision I made, it would change my life forever.

9

A Parade of Suitors

The morning after the Duke's shocking proposal, the entire house buzzed with excitement and anticipation. My parents, especially, were filled with a fervor I had not seen in years, discussing the potential union as though it were already a foregone conclusion. I, however, was far from resigned to my fate.

The weight of Duke Bastian's proposal hung over me like a dark cloud, and the uncertainty gnawed at me. How could I make a decision when the very thought of marrying a man like him sent shivers down my spine? The solution, or at least a temporary distraction, presented itself to me as I sat quietly through yet another conversation between my parents about the advantages of such a prestigious match.

"Mother, Father," I began hesitantly, interrupting their excited chatter. They both turned to look at me, their expressions expectant. "Would it be possible... I mean, before making any decisions about the Duke's proposal... Could I meet other potential suitors?"

Their reaction was a mixture of surprise and confusion. My mother blinked at me, her delicate eyebrows arching in surprise. "Other suitors, Adelaide?"

"Yes," I said, gathering my courage. "I think it would be wise to consider all my options before making such a life-altering decision."

Father frowned, clearly puzzled. "But, Adelaide, why? The Duke of Lightwood is one of the most powerful men in the kingdom. Surely, you're not... displeased with his proposal?"

I forced a smile, trying to mask my true feelings. "No, of course not. It's just that... well, I've never had the chance to truly meet other gentlemen. Perhaps if I did, I could make a more informed decision. After all, a marriage should be based on more than just a title."

My mother exchanged a glance with Father, and for a moment, I feared they might refuse. But then she sighed and gave a small nod. "Very well, Adelaide. If it will ease your mind, we will arrange for you to meet some other eligible gentlemen. But do remember," she added, her tone firm, "that few, if any, can match the status and wealth of the Duke."

"Thank you, Mother. Thank you, Father," I replied, relieved that they hadn't outright dismissed my request. Perhaps, I thought, meeting other suitors would help me find some clarity. Or, at the very least, provide a distraction from the overwhelming pressure of the Duke's proposal.

The following days were a blur of preparations, as my parents made arrangements to invite several eligible gentlemen to our home. I found myself caught between nervous anticipation and growing dread, wondering what this parade of suitors would bring.

The first to arrive was Lord Percival Wentworth, a baron known for his handsome face and impeccable sense of fashion. My mother could barely contain her excitement as she introduced us in the drawing room, her eyes sparkling with hope.

Lord Percival was, indeed, strikingly handsome, with perfectly coiffed hair and a wardrobe that seemed to have been chosen with meticulous care. He smiled at me, his teeth impossibly white, and bowed with exaggerated flourish.

"Miss Blair, a pleasure," he said smoothly, his voice oozing charm.

"The pleasure is mine, Lord Wentworth," I replied politely, though I found his overly polished appearance somewhat off-putting.

As we sat together and engaged in conversation, it quickly became apparent that Lord Percival was far more interested in himself than in anything I had to say. He prattled on about his latest wardrobe choices, the tailor who crafted his suits, and the lengths he went to maintain his perfect appearance.

"And of course," he said, inspecting his reflection in the silver tea tray as if he might spot a hair out of place, "one must always present oneself in the best possible light. After all, appearances are everything in society."

I nodded politely, though inwardly, I was already disenchanted. His vanity was suffocating, and despite his good looks, I found myself increasingly uninterested in what he had to say. By the time our conversation concluded, I was thoroughly relieved to see him go, despite the disappointed look on my mother's face.

The next suitor to arrive was Sir Alfred Brightwell, a wealthy landowner known for his extensive properties in the countryside. Unlike Lord Percival, Sir Alfred was not particularly concerned with fashion or appearance. In fact, he seemed far more concerned with the intricacies of crop rotation and sheep breeding.

"Miss Blair," he greeted me with a curt nod, his voice a low, monotone rumble. "I trust you are interested in the agricultural developments in our fair country?"

"Oh, of course," I replied, attempting to sound enthusiastic as we took our seats in the parlor. "Agriculture is quite important, isn't it?"

"Indeed," he said, his expression serious. "I have recently introduced a new breed of sheep on my estate. They're quite remarkable—larger, more resilient to disease, and with the softest wool you've ever felt. I could spend hours discussing their various merits."

And so he did. For what felt like an eternity, Sir Alfred spoke at length about his sheep, his crops, and the state of his land. I nodded and smiled where appropriate, but my thoughts drifted as he droned on, my interest waning with every passing minute. Sir Alfred was undoubtedly knowledgeable, but his single-minded focus on agriculture left little room for anything else, and I soon found myself longing for a change of subject.

When the conversation finally came to an end, I felt a sense of relief wash over me. Though Sir Alfred was kind and well-meaning, his conversation had been dull and lifeless, leaving me yearning for something more engaging.

The third suitor, Mr. Edgar Tolbert, was a well-known gentleman with a reputation for his impressive intellect and love of literature. I was hopeful that our shared interest in reading might spark a connection, but it quickly became apparent that Mr. Tolbert's love of books far surpassed any interest he had in me.

"Miss Blair," he began as we sat down in the library, "have you read the latest treatise on ancient philosophy? It's an absolute masterpiece, truly enlightening."

"I can't say I have," I admitted, "but I would love to hear more about it."

Mr. Tolbert's eyes lit up, and for the next hour, he spoke passionately about the works of long-dead philosophers, quoting passages in their original languages and debating their finer points with himself. I tried to keep up, but his rapid shifts between topics left me feeling dizzy and overwhelmed. It was clear that Mr. Tolbert was more interested in his own thoughts than in hearing anything I might have to say.

By the time he departed, I was exhausted, my head swimming with abstract concepts and philosophical arguments that I could barely comprehend. I sighed, sinking into a chair in the parlor as I contemplated the string of suitors I had met.

Each one had been more disappointing than the last—Lord Percival, with his vanity; Sir Alfred, with his tedious agricultural talk; and Mr. Tolbert, with his overwhelming intellect. None of them had stirred anything within me, and I couldn't help but feel disheartened.

As I sat there, my thoughts wandered back to Duke Bastian. He, at least, had not been boring, nor vain, nor entirely self-absorbed. There was something about him—something I couldn't quite place—that intrigued me, despite my fear of him. But could I truly see myself as his wife, standing beside him as the Duchess of Lightwood?

My mother entered the room, her expression a mixture of hope and concern. "Adelaide, darling, how are you feeling? Did any of the gentlemen catch your interest?"

I shook my head slowly, forcing a smile. "They were all... very kind, but I don't think any of them are quite what I'm looking for."

She sighed, her shoulders slumping slightly. "I understand, dear. It's difficult to find the right match, especially when we have such high expectations.

But don't lose hope—we'll find someone suitable."

"Thank you, Mother," I said, though my heart was heavy with doubt. Was I being too picky? Too idealistic? Or was I simply afraid of what lay ahead?

As I retired to my chambers that evening, I couldn't shake the feeling that my search for a suitable match was leading me in circles. Each suitor seemed to highlight the growing dissatisfaction I felt with what society expected of me—marriage to a man based on wealth, status, or convenience, rather than love or true connection.

And yet, the Duke's proposal loomed large in my mind, a reminder that my options were limited, and time was running out. I needed to make a decision, but with every passing day, the choice seemed only to grow more complicated.

I lay in bed that night, staring at the ceiling as the faces of my suitors danced in my mind. None of them had been right, but could I truly walk away from a proposal as grand as the Duke's? The question haunted me, leaving me restless and uncertain.

10

A Return from the Past

The days following the parade of disappointing suitors were filled with a restlessness I couldn't seem to shake. My parents, though supportive, were beginning to show signs of concern over my reluctance to accept any of the matches presented to me. The Duke's proposal still loomed large in my mind, an ever-present shadow that I couldn't escape, no matter how hard I tried.

But just as I was beginning to believe that my life had become an endless cycle of decisions I didn't want to make, a familiar figure from my past suddenly reappeared, bringing with him a flood of memories and emotions I wasn't prepared to confront.

Colin, the Marquess of Ashford, had returned to town.

The news of his return reached me one bright afternoon as I was taking tea with my mother in the drawing room. It was Anne who burst in with the announcement, her cheeks flushed with excitement.

"Adelaide, you won't believe it!" she exclaimed, barely able to contain her enthusiasm. "Colin's back in town! He arrived this morning and has already asked to call on us."

I looked up from my teacup, my heart giving a little jolt at the mention of his name. Colin, my childhood friend, my first love, the man who had unwittingly broken my heart so many times over the years. But now, as his name hung in the air, I realized with a start that the feelings I once had for him had changed—had faded, even.

Mother's eyes lit up with interest. "The Marquess of Ashford? How delightful! We must invite him for dinner. Adelaide, you must be thrilled."

I managed a smile, though it felt hollow. "Yes, it will be nice to see him again."

But even as I said the words, I felt a strange sense of detachment. Colin had been a constant in my life, a figure I had once adored with the fervor of young, unrequited love. Yet now, after everything that had happened—the Duke's proposal, the string of unsuitable suitors, the burden of secrets I carried—Colin seemed almost... insignificant.

Still, there was no avoiding him. Later that afternoon, he arrived at our home, his familiar presence filling the drawing room as if he had never been away. He was as handsome as ever, with his easy smile and charming demeanor, but as he greeted me, I realized that something had shifted between us. The butterflies that used to flutter in my stomach at the sight of him were gone, replaced by a dull, uneasy feeling I couldn't quite place.

"Adelaide," he said warmly, taking my hand in his. "It's been too long. You look as lovely as ever."

"Thank you, Colin," I replied, trying to ignore the way his touch no longer sent a thrill through me. "It's good to see you."

We sat together, exchanging pleasantries and catching up on the time he had been away. But the conversation felt forced, as if we were both trying too hard to recapture the ease we had once shared. There was an awkwardness between us that hadn't been there before, and it left me feeling unsettled.

Colin, however, seemed oblivious to the change. He spoke of his travels, his plans for the future, and the latest gossip from the ton, all with the same enthusiasm he had always possessed. But as he talked, I found myself drifting, my thoughts returning to the turmoil I had been facing—the Duke's proposal, the suitors, the secret I could never reveal.

It wasn't until Colin mentioned hearing that I had been meeting suitors that I was jolted back to the present.

"I hear you've been quite the sought-after lady since I've been gone," he said with a teasing smile. "Meeting suitors left and right, are you?"

The comment was meant in jest, a lighthearted remark that would have once made me laugh. But instead, a surge of irritation welled up within me, surprising even myself.

"What do you care, Colin?" I snapped, my tone sharper than I intended. "You've never been interested in me that way before. Why start now?"

Colin blinked, clearly taken aback by my outburst. "Adelaide, I was only joking. There's no need to—"

"Of course you were joking," I interrupted, unable to keep the bitterness from my voice. "That's all it's ever been with you, hasn't it? A joke, a game. But this is my life, Colin. My future."

He stared at me, confusion and hurt flickering in his eyes. "Adelaide, what's gotten into you? I didn't mean to upset you."

I sighed, suddenly weary. The anger that had flared so unexpectedly drained away, leaving behind a deep sense of frustration. How could I explain to him that the girl he had known was no longer the woman sitting before him? That I had been through too much, seen too much, to play the games we used to play?

"You didn't upset me," I said more softly, my eyes avoiding his. "But things have changed, Colin. I've changed."

He frowned, leaning forward as if trying to understand. "What do you mean?"

I hesitated, struggling to find the right words. "I mean... you don't know what I've been through, what I'm dealing with right now. You've been away, living your life, while I've been here, trying to navigate a world that makes less and less sense to me every day."

Colin reached out to take my hand again, his expression earnest. "Adelaide, if something's wrong, you can tell me. I want to help."

I shook my head, gently pulling my hand from his grasp. "You can't help me, Colin. And honestly, I don't think you would want to."

He looked at me, clearly hurt by my words. "How can you say that? You've always been important to me."

"But not important enough," I said quietly, my voice tinged with a sadness I hadn't realized I felt. "You never saw me as anything more than a friend,

Colin. And that's fine. But now, things are different. I'm different. And I can't keep pretending that everything is the same between us."

The room fell into an uncomfortable silence, the air thick with unspoken words. Colin looked down at his hands, his brow furrowed in thought. For the first time since he had arrived, he seemed at a loss for what to say.

Finally, he looked up at me, his eyes searching mine. "What are you saying, Adelaide? That we can't even be friends anymore?"

I hesitated, the weight of my words pressing down on me. "I'm saying that I don't think you understand what I'm going through, Colin. And until you do, maybe it's best if we keep our distance."

His confusion deepened, but he nodded slowly, clearly trying to respect my wishes even if he didn't fully understand them. "If that's what you want, Adelaide."

"It's what I need," I corrected gently, offering him a small, sad smile. "I hope you can understand that."

He nodded again, though the hurt in his eyes was unmistakable. "I'll... I'll leave you be, then. But if you ever want to talk, Adelaide, you know where to find me."

"Thank you, Colin," I said, my voice barely above a whisper.

With that, he stood and bowed, the movement stiff and formal, so different from the carefree Colin I had known. He left the room without another word, leaving me alone with my thoughts.

As the door closed behind him, I felt a pang of sadness, a sense of loss for the friendship we had once shared. But more than that, I felt a strange sense of relief. For the first time, I had faced Colin without the rose-colored glasses of unrequited love, and in doing so, I had realized something important:

The girl who had pined for Colin was gone. In her place stood a woman who had seen too much, who had been through too much, to settle for anything less than what she truly deserved.

11

The Strain of Friendship

The days that followed Colin's return were fraught with an uncomfortable tension that seemed to linger in the air whenever we were together. Our once easy companionship had become strained, our conversations stilted and awkward. Colin, who had always been able to coax a smile from me with a simple joke or a well-timed tease, now seemed at a loss for how to approach me.

And how could he not be? Everything between us had changed, and yet, I couldn't bring myself to explain why. The truth was too complicated, too intertwined with secrets I couldn't share—not with him, not with anyone.

Colin continued to visit, as he always had, but each time he did, the tension between us grew thicker. I could see the confusion in his eyes, the hurt he tried to mask behind his usual charm. But the more he tried to bridge the growing gap, the more I pulled away, retreating into myself.

One afternoon, as we walked through the gardens, the conversation drifted once again into uncomfortable territory. Colin, clearly sensing that something was amiss, turned to me with a frown.

"Adelaide, have I done something to upset you?" he asked, his voice tinged with genuine concern.

I shook my head, avoiding his gaze. "No, Colin, you haven't."

"Then what is it?" he pressed. "You've been so distant lately. We used to be able to talk about anything, but now... it feels like you're keeping something from me."

I hesitated, struggling to find the right words. How could I explain that the very nature of our friendship had changed, that I could no longer see him the way I once had? That my life had taken a turn so unexpected that I could hardly make sense of it myself?

"It's not you, Colin," I said softly, staring at the ground. "It's just... things are different now."

"Different how?" he asked, his frown deepening.

I took a deep breath, steeling myself for what I had to say. "We're not children anymore, Colin. We're adults, and with that comes responsibilities. You're a marquess now, and I... I have decisions to make about my future."

He looked at me, a mixture of confusion and hurt in his eyes. "Adelaide, I know that. But that doesn't mean we have to stop being friends."

I finally met his gaze, my heart heavy with the knowledge that our friendship could never be the same. "Maybe not," I said quietly. "But I think it does mean that we can't keep pretending things haven't changed."

"Pretending?" he echoed, clearly not understanding.

I sighed, feeling the weight of the words I needed to say. "Colin, we can't keep playing the way we used to, spending time together like we're still children. You have a duty to your title, and I have a duty to my family to find a suitable match. It's time we both start taking that seriously."

Colin stared at me, as if seeing me for the first time. "Is that what this is about? Marriage? You're pushing me away because you think we're too old to be friends?"

I nodded, though the words felt hollow in my chest. "Yes. It's time for us to grow up, Colin. We can't keep holding onto the past."

His expression darkened, a flash of frustration crossing his features. "Is that really how you feel? That our friendship is just... childish?"

I looked away, unable to bear the hurt in his eyes. "I think it's time we focus on what's important."

He was silent for a long moment, the tension between us thick and suffocating. Finally, he spoke, his voice tight with emotion. "If that's what you want, Adelaide, then I won't stand in your way. But I'll tell you this—I've never thought of our friendship as childish. It's always meant something to me. I hope it meant something to you, too."

The pain in his voice cut through me like a knife, but I forced myself to remain firm. "It did, Colin. It does. But things are different now, and we need to accept that."

He nodded slowly, though I could see the hurt lingering in his eyes. "Very well. If this is how it has to be..."

Without another word, he turned and walked away, leaving me standing alone in the garden, the distance between us greater than it had ever been.

Later that evening, Anne found me in my room, sitting by the window and staring out at the darkening sky. She had noticed the change in my mood, the tension that had arisen between Colin and me, and she was clearly worried.

"Adelaide," she began, her voice gentle as she sat down beside me. "What's going on with you and Colin? You two have always been so close, but lately... it's like there's something wrong between you."

I sighed, my shoulders slumping as I leaned back in the chair. "It's nothing, Anne. We're just... growing apart, that's all."

"Growing apart?" she echoed, her brow furrowing in confusion. "But why? You two have been inseparable for years."

I hesitated, unsure how much to say. "We're 21 now, Anne. We can't keep having childish friendships forever. It's time to focus on what's important— finding a husband, securing our futures."

Anne looked at me, her confusion deepening. "But you've never been interested in marriage before. You've always said you wanted to take your time, to find someone you truly care about. Why the sudden change?"

I shook my head, not wanting to delve into the complicated emotions swirling within me. "Things change, Anne. People change."

She studied me for a moment, as if trying to decipher the hidden meaning behind my words. But when she spoke again, her tone was soft, understanding. "If you need to talk, Adelaide, I'm here. You don't have to go through this alone."

"Thank you, Anne," I murmured, grateful for her support but unwilling to burden her with the turmoil I was facing. "I'll be fine. I just... need some time to figure things out."

She nodded, reaching out to squeeze my hand. "Take all the time you need. Just remember, you don't have to do this by yourself."

With that, she left the room, leaving me alone with my thoughts once more. The weight of my decisions pressed down on me, the strain of my friendship with Colin adding to the already overwhelming burden I carried.

As I sat by the window, watching the stars appear in the night sky, I couldn't help but wonder if I had made the right choice. Had I pushed Colin away out of fear, out of a desire to protect myself from the pain of unrequited love? Or was I simply trying to distance myself from a friendship that no longer fit the person I was becoming?

12

A Stain on the Page

The estate of Lightwood Hall stood tall and imposing on the crest of a hill, its stone walls as weathered and enduring as the legacy it represented. The manor was a sprawling edifice of wealth and power, every inch of it steeped in centuries of history. The gray stones that made up the exterior bore the weight of countless generations, each one having added to the grandeur of the place. Ivy clung to the walls, as though it sought to hold onto the power within. The gardens stretched out in meticulously designed patterns, a testament to the care and precision that ruled every aspect of life at Lightwood Hall. The hedges were trimmed to perfection, the flowers in bloom a riot of color against the muted tones of the manor.

Inside, the halls were filled with an air of cold elegance. Polished marble floors reflected the light from crystal chandeliers that hung from ceilings painted with scenes of myth and legend. Rich tapestries depicting battles long won adorned the walls, and every room was furnished with the finest materials—silk, velvet, mahogany, and gold leaf. It was a place of impeccable taste, where every item had its place, and nothing was out of order.

But despite its magnificence, the manor had an undeniable air of solitude, a grand but hollow shell that echoed with the footsteps of the past. It had been this way ever since the carriage accident that had claimed the lives of my parents, leaving me the sole heir to a legacy I had never asked for.

This afternoon, however, my thoughts were not on the grandeur of my surroundings, but on a far more vexing matter. I sat at my desk, staring in frustration at the ink that had spilled across the page. The quill in my hand trembled slightly, and I cursed under my breath as I realized that yet another letter had been ruined by my unsteady hand.

"Damn it," I muttered, tossing the quill aside and leaning back in my chair. The once pristine parchment was now marred by a black stain that spread like a blot of corruption, a mirror of my own turbulent thoughts.

Adelaide Blair. The name that had consumed my thoughts since that fateful night, the name that had driven me to take a step I had never imagined myself taking—proposing marriage. I had never been one to entertain notions of love or passion, but with her, everything had changed.

It had all started with a single night, a night that should have been forgotten in the haze of wine and reckless abandon. But Adelaide had been different. Her kiss, her touch, her whispered words—they had burrowed deep into my mind, refusing to let go. She had taken something from me that night, something I had never given to another. And then, without a word, she had vanished, as if the entire encounter had meant nothing to her.

But it had meant something to me. Damn it, it had meant everything. I couldn't erase her from my mind, no matter how hard I tried. Her memory haunted me, her absence gnawing at me like a wound that refused to heal. And so, I had made the decision to seek her out, to make her mine in the only way I knew how—by proposing marriage.

But days had passed since I had sent the letter, and there had been no reply. The silence was unbearable, a constant reminder of the uncertainty that now plagued me.

With a growl of irritation, I reached for the bell on my desk and rang it sharply. Moments later, Alfred, my ever-faithful butler, appeared in the doorway, his expression calm and composed as always. He was a man of few words, but he understood me better than most, having served my family since I was a child.

"My lord?" Alfred inquired, his voice steady and respectful.

"Alfred," I began, trying to keep the frustration from my voice. "Has there been any word from Miss Blair? Any reply to my letter?"

Alfred inclined his head slightly, his expression unchanging. "I regret to inform you, my lord, that no reply has yet been received. However, it is possible that the response is on its way and has simply not yet arrived at the manor."

I frowned, my fingers drumming impatiently on the edge of the desk. "It's been days, Alfred. The silence is... unsettling."

"Indeed, my lord," Alfred agreed, though his tone was as neutral as ever. "Perhaps Miss Blair is simply taking her time to consider such an important matter."

"Or perhaps she's avoiding it altogether," I muttered darkly, though the very thought was an affront to my pride. The idea that Adelaide could simply brush off what had happened between us, that she could act as if that night had never occurred, was infuriating. I had never been a man to dwell on emotions, but with her, everything was different.

Damn her for getting under my skin.

I clenched my fists, the memory of her warm body pressed against mine, the way her lips had moved against mine with such urgency, flashing through my mind. I had been unprepared for the intensity of it all, the way she had consumed me so completely in such a short span of time. And then she had disappeared, leaving me alone in that bed, her scent still lingering in the air, her presence a ghost that haunted me long after she had gone.

Alfred, ever perceptive, seemed to sense my unease. "If I may, my lord," he ventured, "Miss Blair is known for her thoughtful nature. It is likely that she is simply weighing the gravity of your proposal."

"Thoughtful," I repeated, a wry smile tugging at the corner of my mouth. "A polite way of saying she's hesitant, I suppose."

Alfred's expression remained impassive. "Miss Blair is an intelligent young woman. She will consider all aspects before making her decision."

I nodded, though my mind was still restless. Alfred's words were sensible, but they did little to quell the frustration that simmered beneath the surface. I was a man who dealt in certainties, in control, and the uncertainty surrounding Adelaide's response was a thorn in my side.

"Very well," I said finally, dismissing the matter with a wave of my hand.

"Keep me informed the moment any correspondence arrives."

"Of course, my lord," Alfred replied with a bow, before retreating from the room, leaving me alone with my thoughts once more.

I stared down at the ruined letter on my desk, the ink slowly drying into a permanent stain on the page. It was a small thing, a minor inconvenience, but it felt like a harbinger of something larger, something I couldn't quite put my finger on.

Adelaide Blair. The name echoed in my mind, accompanied by the memory of that night—the way she had looked at me with those hazel eyes, the way her laughter had filled the room, the way her touch had set my blood on fire. She was everything I wasn't—warm, open, full of life—and perhaps that was why I couldn't forget her.

But it was more than that. She had taken something from me, something I had never given to anyone, and she had done it without a second thought, leaving me to grapple with the aftermath on my own. And I, the man who had always prided himself on being in control, had been left in a state of chaos ever since.

It wasn't just that she had taken my virginity. It was the way she had done it—the way she had claimed me so completely, so effortlessly, as if it were the most natural thing in the world. And then she had walked away, leaving me with nothing but the memory of her touch, her kiss, her whispered words.

I clenched my fists, the frustration and anger I had tried to suppress bubbling to the surface. I had never been one to lose my composure, but with Adelaide, everything was different. I wanted her, needed her, in a way that I couldn't explain. And the thought that she might not feel the same, that she might be content to forget that night ever happened, was unbearable.

But she would remember. She had to. And if she thought she could simply erase me from her mind, she was sorely mistaken.

I shook my head, forcing myself to focus on the tasks at hand. There was no sense in dwelling on what might be. I had made my proposal, and now the decision rested with Adelaide.

But I wouldn't wait forever. Sooner or later, she would have to face me. And when she did, she would see that I was not a man to be forgotten.

13

A Royal Predicament

I had always considered myself a man of great patience—measured, controlled, unfazed by the whims of those around me. But this morning, as I stared at the empty silver tray where Miss Adelaide Blair's reply should have been, I realized that patience was a virtue I was rapidly losing.

"Alfred!" I called, my voice sharper than I intended. The irritation that had been simmering beneath the surface since my letter was sent had finally boiled over. Moments later, Alfred appeared in the doorway, his expression as calm and composed as ever.

"Yes, my lord?" he inquired, his tone polite, as though he hadn't just seen me glaring daggers at the innocent tray.

"Still nothing?" I asked, though the answer was clear. The damn tray was empty, and had been for days. The silence from Miss Blair was growing unbearable. "No word from Miss Blair?"

Alfred's eyes flicked to the tray, and I could have sworn I saw a flicker of amusement cross his usually impassive face. "I'm afraid not, my lord."

I clenched my jaw, forcing myself to remain calm. "What could possibly be taking so long? It's been days, Alfred. Days."

Alfred, ever the master of understatement, nodded sagely. "Indeed, my lord. It is rather curious."

"Curious?" I echoed, my frustration mounting. "It's downright maddening. Has she forgotten how to write? Is she deliberately ignoring me?"

Alfred remained unruffled. "It is possible, my lord, that Miss Blair is simply considering your proposal with great care."

I frowned, the words doing little to soothe my irritation. "Or perhaps she's just tossing my letter into the fire and laughing about it with her friends."

Alfred raised an eyebrow, a hint of a smile tugging at the corners of his mouth. "That is also a possibility, my lord."

"Not helping, Alfred," I muttered, running a hand through my hair in frustration. The thought of Adelaide laughing at my proposal, dismissing it as some sort of joke, made my blood boil. And yet, the idea that she might be genuinely hesitant—perhaps even rejecting me—was worse.

Alfred, sensing my darkening mood, offered a suggestion with an air of casual indifference that only he could pull off. "Perhaps, my lord, she is preparing a very lengthy and detailed reply. One that requires careful thought and consideration."

I scowled. "Or perhaps she's simply trying to avoid the inevitable."

"The inevitable, my lord?" Alfred's tone was impeccably polite, but I could see the glint in his eye.

"Yes, Alfred. The inevitable. Her acceptance of my proposal," I said, though the confidence in my words felt increasingly hollow with each passing day.

Alfred, bless him, decided to press on with his theories. "Of course, my lord. But on the off chance that she is, shall we say, less than inclined to accept...?"

I shot him a glare. "You mean if she's planning to reject me."

"Perish the thought, my lord," Alfred said smoothly. "But if, hypothetically, such an outcome were to occur, it would be prudent to consider alternative measures."

"Alternative measures?" I repeated, intrigued despite my irritation. "Such as?"

"Well," Alfred began, his tone suggesting he was about to say something utterly ridiculous, "there is always the option of applying for a royal decree."

I blinked, caught off guard by the suggestion. "A royal decree? You mean... force her to reply?"

Alfred inclined his head slightly, his expression perfectly composed. "Or perhaps even better, my lord, you could request a royal decree for marriage.

55

After all, if a mere letter is being ignored, surely a decree would garner the attention it deserves."

I stared at him, half convinced that he had lost his mind. "A royal decree to marry? That's positively medieval, Alfred."

"Indeed, my lord," Alfred agreed, a twinkle of amusement in his eye. "But effective, nonetheless. A time-honored tradition, one might say. The crown has the power to bestow such orders, and it could certainly eliminate the tiresome wait for a response."

For a moment, I was speechless, the absurdity of the idea clashing with the undeniable appeal of forcing Adelaide's hand. But then, slowly, a smile began to tug at the corners of my mouth. "You're suggesting I bypass the entire courtship process and just... demand her hand?"

Alfred's response was nothing short of dignified. "It would certainly save time, my lord."

The very thought was so outrageous that I couldn't help but laugh, the sound echoing through the vast expanse of my study. "A royal decree to marry Miss Blair. That's a bit extreme, don't you think?"

"Desperate times, my lord," Alfred replied, his voice laced with dry humor. "And I daresay, it would be interesting to see Miss Blair's reaction."

"Oh, it would be interesting, indeed," I mused, the idea taking root in my mind despite its absurdity. The thought of Adelaide's reaction—her sharp wit, her fiery spirit—was enough to make me pause. Would she be furious? Amused? Would she find the whole thing as ridiculous as I did?

Or would she finally take me seriously?

"Hm," I murmured, leaning back in my chair and crossing my arms over my chest. "Marrying by royal decree... old-fashioned, yes. But it could be an intriguing option."

Alfred's expression remained perfectly composed, though I could see the faintest hint of satisfaction in his eyes. "As you say, my lord."

I tapped my fingers on the arm of the chair, considering the possibility. It was, of course, a ridiculous notion—laughable, even. And yet, there was something undeniably appealing about the idea of cutting through the nonsense, the waiting, and simply taking what I wanted. After all, I had never been a man who enjoyed being kept in suspense.

"What do you think, Alfred?" I asked, a glint of mischief in my eye. "Should we draw up the papers?"

Alfred, ever the professional, responded with the utmost seriousness. "If you wish it, my lord, I shall see to it immediately."

I laughed again, the tension that had gripped me for days finally beginning to ease. "No, Alfred. Not yet. Let's give Miss Blair a little more time to come to her senses."

"As you wish, my lord," Alfred replied, a ghost of a smile playing on his lips.

But as he left the room, I found myself still toying with the idea, my mind drifting back to the thought of Adelaide's reaction. She was no simpering debutante, that much was certain. She would undoubtedly have a thing or two to say about being ordered to marry by royal decree.

And the more I thought about it, the more I realized that I was genuinely curious to see what she would do.

"Well, Miss Blair," I murmured to myself, a smirk tugging at my lips. "Let's see how long you can keep me waiting."

14

A Dangerous Proposition

The day began like any other—calm, predictable, and utterly ordinary. The morning sun cast its warm light over Windermere Manor, the gardens bursting with life as the summer blooms reached their peak. I tried to lose myself in a book, to find solace in the familiar, but my thoughts kept drifting to the letter that had arrived days ago—the letter I had no intention of answering. The Duke of Lightwood's proposal had felt like a trap, one I refused to fall into.

The thought of marrying a man like Bastian Lightwood, with his icy demeanor and reputation for ruthlessness, was intolerable. I wanted nothing to do with him, and I hoped my silence would be enough to convey that message.

But fate, it seemed, had other plans.

My peace was shattered when a flustered maid burst into the drawing room, her eyes wide with panic. "Miss Adelaide! The Duke of Lightwood is here! He's just arrived—unannounced!"

I froze, the book slipping from my hands and landing on the floor with a dull thud. "The Duke... here?" My voice sounded distant, as though it belonged to someone else.

"Yes, miss!" the maid replied, wringing her hands nervously. "The staff is in a flurry—your parents are in the front hall preparing to greet him!"

The news hit me like a physical blow. Bastian was here. At Windermere

Manor. And without any warning.

My heart raced as I made my way to the front hall, the sound of my footsteps on the polished floor seeming unnaturally loud. I could hear the low murmur of voices—my mother's warm greeting, my father's more formal tone. And then, as I rounded the corner, I saw him.

Bastian Lightwood, the Duke of Lightwood, stood in the center of the hall, commanding the space with an intimidating presence. He was dressed impeccably, his dark clothes tailored to perfection. His black hair was as neatly combed as his demeanor, and his piercing eyes swept over the room with a gaze that could cut through steel. There was something almost predatory about him, as if he were a lion surveying his domain.

I forced myself to step forward, my pulse quickening. My mother's eyes lit up when she saw me, her expression one of barely contained excitement. "Ah, Adelaide, there you are! The Duke of Lightwood has graced us with an unexpected visit!"

"Yes, I see that," I replied, struggling to keep my voice steady as I curtsied. "Your Grace."

Bastian's eyes met mine, and for a moment, the world seemed to shrink to just the two of us. His gaze was intense, as if he could see straight through me, past the polite facade I was trying so hard to maintain.

"Miss Blair," he said, his voice smooth but carrying an edge. "A pleasure to see you again."

The words were courteous enough, but there was an unspoken tension behind them, a weight that made the air between us thick and charged. My parents were oblivious to the undercurrents, but I could feel them, sharp and unyielding.

"Won't you join us for tea, Your Grace?" my mother offered, her voice brimming with enthusiasm. "It's such a delight to have you here."

Bastian's gaze didn't waver from mine. "I would be honored, Lady Windermere," he replied, though I could tell his focus was entirely on me.

I forced a smile, though my stomach twisted with unease. "Perhaps we should speak privately, Your Grace," I suggested, keeping my tone measured. "I'm sure you have matters to discuss that would be best handled away from prying ears."

My father raised an eyebrow, but before he could object, Bastian nodded. "A wise suggestion, Miss Blair."

My parents exchanged a look, but they knew better than to argue with a duke. With a gracious nod, my mother led the way to the drawing room, where the staff had hastily prepared tea. Once we were seated, my parents began the usual pleasantries, engaging Bastian in conversation about the estate, the weather, and all the mundane topics that society deemed appropriate for such an occasion.

But I could barely focus on their words. I could feel Bastian's eyes on me, watching, waiting. The tension between us was palpable, an invisible thread that tightened with every passing moment. My heart raced, the memory of that night surfacing against my will.

Finally, after what felt like an eternity, my mother rose, a knowing smile on her lips. "If you'll excuse us, Your Grace, I'm sure you and Adelaide would appreciate a moment to speak privately."

I wanted to protest, to beg her to stay, but the words caught in my throat. Bastian merely inclined his head. "Of course, Lady Windermere."

As my parents left the room, the door closing softly behind them, the silence that followed was suffocating. Bastian remained seated, his gaze fixed on me with an intensity that made it hard to breathe.

"Miss Blair," he began, his voice low and controlled, "I believe there is a matter we need to address."

I folded my hands in my lap, forcing myself to meet his gaze. "Indeed, Your Grace. Though I must admit, I'm at a loss as to what you're referring to."

His lips curved into a faint, humorless smile. "You know exactly what I'm referring to, Adelaide."

The sound of my name on his lips sent a shiver down my spine, but I refused to show any sign of weakness. "I assure you, Your Grace, I do not."

Bastian's eyes narrowed slightly, a hint of frustration flickering across his face. "You've been avoiding me."

I raised an eyebrow, feigning innocence. "Avoiding you? Your Grace, we've hardly had any interaction at all."

His gaze darkened, the polite mask slipping for just a moment. "Don't play coy with me, Adelaide. You know very well that I've been waiting for a response to my letter."

Ah, so that's what this was about. The letter. The proposal. I resisted the urge to roll my eyes. "I received your letter, yes. And as I have not responded, I would think that would make my answer quite clear."

"And yet," he said, his voice softening into a dangerous whisper, "ignoring the matter does not resolve it."

I stiffened, my heart skipping a beat. There was something in his tone, something that hinted at knowledge I desperately wished he didn't possess. "I don't see what there is to resolve, Your Grace. We've barely spoken to one another. A proposal of marriage between us makes no sense."

For a moment, Bastian said nothing. Then, slowly, deliberately, he reached into his coat pocket and withdrew something small, something that glinted in the light. My breath caught in my throat as I recognized what it was.

My necklace.

The very necklace I had worn that night. The night I had tried so hard to forget, the night that had haunted me ever since.

"How—" I began, my voice faltering as the sight of it brought back a rush of memories. "So that man was... you?"

Bastian's eyes narrowed, confusion flashing across his face before it hardened into something more menacing. "Stop playing games, Adelaide. You know perfectly well what happened that night."

I shook my head, the weight of the situation crashing down on me. "I swear to you, I didn't know. I—I don't remember everything from that night, and I had no idea it was you."

His expression darkened further, the intensity of his gaze nearly over-whelming. "You don't remember?" he repeated, his voice low and dangerous. "Convenient. But not remembering does not mean it didn't happen."

The room seemed to tilt slightly, the air thick with tension. "I'm telling the truth, Your Grace. I didn't know it was you. I never meant—"

"Your dress is wet, Miss," said a man, his eyes filled with concern as he looked at the soaked fabric clinging to my body. *"I'll have the maid change it."*

As the man was about to leave, I pulled him back and made him sit on the bed. I moved closer and kissed him. "Your lips are wet too, My Lord. May I kiss them again?"

"You asked for it," he said, as he pulled my chin with his hand and crushed my lips with a passion that took her breath away.

I kissed him back, our breaths colliding in a heady mix of desire and need. My heart pounded in my chest as I touched his hard, firm chest.

Our kiss broke, and he dropped me onto the bed, his eyes dark with desire. He squeezed my breasts, his fingers pinching my nipples gently before he bent his head and took one into his mouth, biting it gently.

I moaned, my back arching off the bed as he continued to tease and tantalize my nipples, his tongue tracing lazy circles around my areolas.

"You like that, don't you?" he murmured, his voice husky with desire.

"Yes," I gasped, my hands reaching down to unbutton his pants. "I want you inside me."

He chuckled, his breath warm against my skin. "Patience, my lady. We have all the time in the world."

"But I wanted you right now, My Lord. And..."

And....

I shook my head a few times as the memory flashed.

"This is impossible, we never..."

"Enough," he snapped, cutting me off. His voice was sharp, filled with barely contained anger. "Whether you meant it or not is irrelevant. What matters is that it did happen. And you will take responsibility for it."

"Responsibility?" I echoed, my voice trembling with a mix of fear and anger. "For what? We've barely spoken to each other, and now you're demanding I marry you because of a night I can't even remember?"

Bastian leaned forward, his eyes locking onto mine with a ferocity that made it impossible to look away. "That night, Adelaide, you took something from me that I can never get back. My virginity."

I stared at him, utterly stunned by the revelation. "Your... virginity?" The word felt foreign on my tongue, the implications of it crashing over me like a wave. "But... how—why..."

Bastian's lips curled into a grim smile, though there was no humor in it. "You may not have known, but that doesn't change what happened. And it doesn't change the fact that I refuse to let you walk away from this unscathed."

I could hardly process what I was hearing. The Duke of Lightwood, the man who had become a symbol of cold, unfeeling power, was standing before me, demanding I take responsibility for something that felt like a dream—a nightmare—I could barely remember.

"What do you want from me?" I asked, my voice barely above a whisper.

Bastian's gaze remained unyielding, his voice a low, dangerous murmur. "I want you to marry me, Adelaide. You and I both know that we are tied together by more than just a single night. This isn't about love—it's about accountability. About doing what is right."

"Right?" I scoffed, my anger flaring again despite the fear that gripped me. "There's nothing right about this, Bastian. You're using that night to force my hand, to trap me in a marriage I don't want."

He met my gaze steadily, his tone unyielding. "Perhaps. But you and I both know that running from this won't change what happened. You can deny it all you want, but the truth will come out eventually. Better to face it now, on our terms, than to have it exposed in a way that neither of us can control."

I clenched my fists, my mind racing. The choice he offered was no choice at all—either I agreed to marry him, or he would expose our secret to the world, dragging my name and my family's honor through the mud.

And yet, as much as I hated him in that moment, I couldn't deny that he was right. The truth would come out eventually. And when it did, it would destroy everything I held dear. But I couldn't let him bully me into a decision, not like this. I had to buy myself some time, to think clearly and weigh my options.

I swallowed hard, choosing my words carefully. "I will consider your proposal, but I cannot give you an answer right now. This is a life-changing decision, and I need time to think."

His eyes narrowed slightly, as if he were trying to gauge whether I was stalling or genuinely considering his offer. "How much time do you need?"

"I don't know," I admitted, my voice steadying as I continued. "But I can't be rushed into this. You have to understand—marriage isn't something I can agree to on a whim."

For a moment, he said nothing, his gaze locked onto mine as if searching for some sign of deception. Then, to my surprise, he nodded. "Very well. Take your time. But know this—my patience is not infinite."

I felt a flicker of relief, though it was short-lived. I had expected him to push harder, to insist on an immediate answer, but his unexpected willingness to give me time only made me more uneasy. He was planning something, I could feel it.

Just as I was beginning to think I had bought myself a reprieve, Bastian's expression shifted, a calculating gleam entering his eyes. "Of course, there's something you should consider while you're making up your mind."

I tensed, my instincts warning me that whatever he was about to say would not be good. "What do you mean?"

Bastian stepped closer, his voice dropping to a conspiratorial whisper. "Have you considered the possibility that you might already be carrying my child?"

The words were like a slap to the face. My heart skipped a beat, and I stared at him in disbelief. "What? No, that's impossible!"

But Bastian's smile only widened, a dark, predatory grin that made my skin crawl. "Is it? Are you so certain?"

I shook my head, refusing to let him rattle me. "Yes, I'm certain. It's only been a short time since that night. I would know if something were amiss."

Bastian's gaze remained fixed on me, his smile never faltering. "Would you? Or are you just telling yourself that because it's easier to believe?"

A cold sweat broke out along the back of my neck, but I refused to let him see how much his words were affecting me. "You're bluffing. There's no way you could know something like that."

"Bluffing?" he echoed, his tone mocking. "Adelaide, I was there that night, too. I know what happened between us. I know how... intense it was. And I know that I put my seed inside you, over and over again."

His words sent a shiver of horror down my spine. "Stop it," I whispered, my voice trembling despite my best efforts. "You're trying to scare me."

He took another step closer, his gaze never leaving mine. "Am I? Or am I simply stating the facts? The truth is, Adelaide, you don't know. And until you do, every moment that passes is a moment closer to potential ruin."

My mind raced, the reality of what he was suggesting settling in like a lead weight in my stomach. Could it be possible? Could I be... pregnant? The very thought was terrifying, and yet I knew he was right—I couldn't be sure. Not yet.

"You can't just... make something like that up," I protested weakly, though the doubt was already creeping in.

Bastian's smile faded, replaced by a cold, calculating expression. "I'm not making it up. And if you're wise, you'll consider the possibility very carefully before you decide how to proceed."

He took off his pants, his cock springing free, hard and ready. I reached out, my fingers wrapping around his shaft, and stroked him gently.

"You're so big," I murmured, my eyes wide with wonder.

"And you're so wet," he replied, his fingers sliding into my pussy, easing in and out with practiced ease.

"Oh, God," I moaned, my hips bucking up to meet his fingers. "Please, I need you inside me."

He positioned himself between my legs, his cock nudging at my entrance. "Is this what you want?"

"Yes, please," I gasped, my hands reaching down to grip his hips, pulling him closer.

He thrust into me, filling me completely, and I cried out, my nails digging into his skin.

"Fuck, you feel amazing," he groaned, his hips starting to move in a slow, steady rhythm.

"Harder," I begged, my legs wrapping around his waist, pulling him deeper.

He obliged, his thrusts becoming harder, faster, his cock hitting with every stroke.

"Yes, yes, yes," I chanted, my orgasm building inside me, tightening my muscles, making my breath catch in my throat.

"Come for me, my lady," he growled, his fingers finding my clit, rubbing it in time with his thrusts.

I screamed, the orgasm crashing over me in waves of pleasure so intense I thought I might pass out.

He continued to thrust, his own orgasm building until he couldn't hold back any longer. With a final, deep thrust, he came, his cock pulsing inside me as he filled me with his seed.

We collapsed onto the bed, our bodies slick with sweat, our breaths coming in ragged gasps.

"That was incredible," he murmured, his lips finding my lips in a gentle kiss.

"Yes, it was," I agreed, my fingers tracing idle patterns on his chest.

When the memory came back, I felt a wave of nausea wash over me, my hands trembling at my sides. Bastian was right, he had entered mine that night, over and over again. But the idea of carrying his child—of being tied to him in that way—was too much to bear. And yet, what choice did I have?

I looked up at him, my voice barely above a whisper. "I need time to think."

"Take all the time you need," Bastian said, his voice as smooth as silk. "But remember, the longer you wait, the more the risk grows. Make your decision wisely, Adelaide. Your future depends on it."

With that, he turned and left the room, leaving me standing there in a daze, my thoughts a chaotic swirl of fear, confusion, and disbelief.

I had thought that night was behind me, a terrible mistake that I could put out of my mind and move on from. But Bastian had made it clear that it was far from over. And now, I was faced with an impossible choice—marry him and secure my family's honor, or refuse and risk everything, including the possibility that I might already be carrying his child.

15

The Doubt

After Bastian left, his words echoed in my mind like a haunting refrain. Could I be pregnant? The very idea seemed absurd, and yet... he had spoken with such certainty.

As I paced the confines of my room, I couldn't shake the unease that had settled in the pit of my stomach. It had been over two weeks since that night, and though I had tried to put the whole affair out of my mind, Bastian's insinuation had thrown everything into disarray. Surely, I would know if something were amiss. Surely, there would be signs.

But what did I know about pregnancy, really? I was the youngest in the family, and my older sister, Anne, had always been the one who seemed so knowledgeable about these matters. I had never seen our mother pregnant, and babies were just distant figures in nurseries, carried by nannies and visited on occasion. Pregnancy was something I had never given much thought to.

I found myself standing in front of the mirror, staring at my reflection as if it might offer some kind of answer. My gaze drifted downward, to my stomach. It was a perfectly ordinary stomach, I told myself. And yet...

I rubbed my hand over my abdomen, feeling a flicker of doubt. Was it my imagination, or was it not as flat as it had been? No, surely it was nothing. I had indulged in too many slices of cake at tea, that was all. A little extra cake never hurt anyone, right?

But the nagging thoughts wouldn't leave me alone. I couldn't help but notice that I hadn't gotten my period this month. Normally, I didn't pay much attention to such things—my cycle had never been particularly regular—but now, with Bastian's words hanging over me like a dark cloud, I found myself fixating on it.

Maybe it was just late. That happened sometimes, didn't it? It didn't mean anything. Except... Bastian had been so sure. He had looked me in the eyes and practically dared me to deny it. He had told me that his seed had entered me, and no matter how much I wanted to dismiss it as a crude bluff, I couldn't forget the way he had said it.

The memory of his voice, the dark, confident tone in which he had made that assertion, sent a wave of nausea rolling through me. It was too much to think about, too much to bear.

I shook my head, trying to banish the thought from my mind. I was just overthinking this. That had to be it. But the knot in my stomach tightened, and I found myself moving toward the washroom, my steps quickening as the nausea grew more intense.

Before I knew it, I was on my knees in front of the toilet, vomiting up everything I had eaten that day. My stomach heaved, my body rejecting the very thought of what Bastian had implied. It was as if my mind and body were conspiring against me, making it impossible to ignore the possibility.

When the retching finally subsided, I sat back on my heels, trembling and breathless. The taste of bile lingered in my mouth, a bitter reminder of how far this nightmare had gone.

As I sat there on the cold, tiled floor, the reality of the situation began to sink in, piece by piece. Bastian's voice, so calm and certain, replayed in my mind, and I realized with a jolt that he hadn't just been taunting me. He genuinely believed that I could be pregnant.

Pregnant.

I looked down at my stomach again, my hand trembling as I pressed it against the slight curve. It was ridiculous, wasn't it? There was nothing there—nothing but the remnants of my own anxiety and too much cake. And yet... why hadn't my cycle come this month? Why had I felt so nauseous all of a sudden?

Why had Bastian seemed so confident?

A fresh wave of fear washed over me, and I struggled to my feet, gripping the edge of the washbasin for support. I needed to clear my head, to stop this spiral of panic before it consumed me. But the more I tried to calm myself, the more the doubt crept in, insidious and unrelenting.

I splashed cold water on my face, the icy sting momentarily shocking me out of my thoughts. I took a deep breath, trying to steady myself. I was overreacting. That had to be it. I was letting Bastian get under my skin, letting his cruel words twist my thoughts into something dark and terrifying.

But even as I tried to convince myself, I couldn't shake the growing sense of dread. The truth was, I didn't know. I didn't know what was happening to my body, and that uncertainty was eating away at me.

I needed to talk to someone. Someone who could help me make sense of this. But who? My mother? No, I couldn't burden her with this—she would be horrified, and I couldn't bear to see the disappointment in her eyes. Anne? She was older, wiser, and more experienced, but how could I tell her about this? The thought of seeing her look at me with pity—or worse, with judgment— was unbearable.

No, I couldn't confide in my family. But maybe... maybe I could ask someone else, someone who wouldn't suspect anything. My thoughts turned to Betsy, our maid. Betsy had been with our family for years, and she was practical, down-to-earth, and had a way of making even the most dire situations seem manageable. She might know something about pregnancy, and I could ask her without revealing too much.

Making up my mind, I wiped my face with a towel and straightened my dress. I couldn't afford to let anyone else see me in this state. With as much composure as I could muster, I left the washroom and headed downstairs to find Betsy.

The manor was quiet, the household settling into the late afternoon calm. I found Betsy in the kitchen, overseeing the preparations for dinner. She looked up as I entered, a warm smile on her face.

"Miss Adelaide, is everything all right?" she asked, her tone concerned as she took in my pale face.

I forced a smile, trying to keep my voice steady. "Oh, yes, Betsy. I was just curious about something and thought you might know."

Betsy's expression softened with concern, and she set down the spoon she had been using to stir a pot. "Of course, miss. What would you like to know?"

I hesitated, trying to find the right way to phrase my question. I couldn't just come out and ask if I was pregnant—that would be far too suspicious. Instead, I opted for a more general approach. "I was wondering... what are the signs of pregnancy? You know, the early ones?"

Betsy's brow furrowed slightly, but she didn't press me on why I was asking. "Well, miss, there are a few signs. Missing your monthly cycle is one of the first, along with nausea, especially in the mornings. Some women notice their bodies changing—tenderness in certain areas, or a bit of swelling around the stomach. But it's different for everyone."

I nodded, my mind racing as I took in her words. Everything she had mentioned... it was everything I had been experiencing. But it couldn't be. It just couldn't.

"Is it... common for those signs to appear right away?" I asked, trying to keep my voice casual.

"It depends, miss," Betsy replied, her tone thoughtful. "Some women notice changes almost immediately, while others don't realize until much later. It's different for everyone."

I felt a lump forming in my throat, but I forced it down, nodding again. "I see. Thank you, Betsy. I was just... curious."

Betsy smiled warmly, though I could see the curiosity in her eyes. "Of course, miss. If you have any more questions, you know where to find me."

I thanked her and quickly excused myself, the weight of her words pressing down on me like a leaden blanket. As I made my way back to my room, I couldn't shake the growing sense of dread. The signs were there, as clear as day, and I had tried so hard to ignore them. But I couldn't ignore them any longer.

The reflection in the mirror greeted me again as I returned, my thoughts a tangled mess. I pressed my hand to my stomach once more, staring at the faint curve that I wasn't sure had been there before. It was too early to know, too early to be sure of anything. But the doubt had taken root, and I knew it would only grow.

And Bastian's voice echoed in my mind once more, calm, confident, and unshakable.

Could he be right?

16

A Family Discussion

The night was oppressive, the darkness of my room mirroring the turmoil in my mind. Sleep eluded me as thoughts of Bastian's words twisted and churned in my head, refusing to let me rest. The possibility of pregnancy hung over me like a storm cloud, dark and foreboding, threatening to shatter everything I had ever known.

What would I do if I truly was with child? The question gnawed at me relentlessly, an unanswerable riddle that left me paralyzed with fear. The thought of telling Bastian was unthinkable—I couldn't bring myself to admit to him, of all people, that his cruel insinuations had taken root in my heart. But if it were true, if I were truly carrying his child... what then?

Would I marry him, as he so coldly demanded? The idea made my skin crawl, but could I truly refuse if it meant preserving my family's honor? Yet, how could I live with myself, bound to a man I hardly knew, a man who wielded his power like a weapon? A man who had all but blackmailed me into submission with the mere possibility of my pregnancy?

And if I refused him, if I chose to keep the pregnancy hidden... was that even possible? The scandal would be enormous, the shame unbearable. How could my family hide such a thing? How could I, with a growing belly and a secret too large to conceal?

Every path I considered seemed to lead to disaster, each choice worse than the last. I tossed and turned, the weight of my decisions pressing down on me like an iron shackle. What was I to do?

By morning, I was no closer to an answer, my exhaustion only heightening the anxiety that had taken hold of me. I had barely touched the breakfast laid out before me, and when Anne suggested a walk in the gardens to clear my head, I could only nod in agreement, hoping the fresh air might provide some clarity.

But my reprieve was short-lived. As we made our way back inside, I noticed my mother and father in quiet conversation, their expressions serious. It wasn't long before my mother turned to me, her eyes lighting up with a mixture of excitement and determination that sent a shiver down my spine.

"Adelaide, we need to discuss something important," she said, her tone indicating that this was not a request.

I knew what was coming before the words even left her lips. The Duke's proposal. The very thought of it sent a fresh wave of panic through me, but I forced myself to remain calm, to follow my parents to the drawing room where the family had gathered.

Anne was there, her usual warm smile replaced with a look of curiosity and concern. My father stood by the fireplace, his posture stiff, his expression grave. The air in the room was thick with expectation, and I knew there would be no escaping this conversation.

"Adelaide," my father began, his voice steady but firm, "the Duke of Lightwood's proposal is a significant one. It is not something we can take lightly."

I nodded, unable to find my voice. I knew what was coming, the pressure that would be placed upon me, but I wasn't prepared for the weight of it, not after the sleepless night I'd endured.

My mother's eyes softened as she looked at me, her tone gentler than my father's. "My dear, this is an incredible opportunity. The Duke is a powerful man, well-respected, and this marriage would secure your future in ways we could never have imagined."

"Mother, I understand," I said, my voice trembling despite my best efforts to remain composed. "But... I don't know if I'm ready to make such a decision. This is my life we're talking about."

My father frowned, his expression stern. "Adelaide, you're a grown woman. It's time to consider your future seriously. The Duke's proposal is not something you can afford to dismiss out of hand. He is offering you stability, security, and a place in one of the most prestigious families in the country."

I looked to Anne, hoping for some support, but her face was unreadable, her eyes flicking between our parents and me as if she were weighing her own thoughts. Finally, she spoke, her voice measured. "Adelaide, I know this must be difficult for you. But Father is right—this is an extraordinary match. It's not just about you; it's about our family, our standing. Marrying the Duke would bring us great honor."

Their words were like stones being placed upon my chest, each one heavier than the last. How could they understand what I was feeling? How could they know the fear that gripped me, the terror of what might already be growing inside me?

But I couldn't tell them. I couldn't admit to the possibility that Bastian's cruel words might be true, that I might already be carrying his child. How could I? The shame would be unbearable, the scandal unthinkable.

"I... I just need time to think," I stammered, my heart racing. "Please, I need to consider this carefully."

My mother's expression softened further, but I could see the determination in her eyes. "Of course, dear. But don't take too long. The Duke won't wait forever."

My father nodded in agreement. "This is not a decision to be delayed. We expect you to give it serious thought, Adelaide."

"I will," I promised, though the words felt hollow, insincere. How could I possibly make such a decision with so much uncertainty hanging over me?

The conversation shifted, but I barely heard the rest of what was said. My thoughts were consumed by the possibilities that loomed before me, each one more terrifying than the last. Could I marry Bastian to save my family's reputation, even if it meant sacrificing my own happiness? Or could I find a way to hide the truth, to keep my secrets buried and hope that they would never see the light of day?

But deep down, I knew the answer. If I truly was pregnant, there would be no hiding it. Bastian would know, and the world would know soon after. The shame, the scandal—it would destroy everything I had ever known.

And yet, the alternative was just as unbearable. To marry a man like Bastian, a man who had forced my hand with his cruel insinuations, was a fate I couldn't bring myself to accept.

But what choice did I have?

The room began to close in around me, the walls pressing in with the weight of my family's expectations, the crushing pressure of the decision I had to make. I could feel their eyes on me, waiting for my response, waiting for me to do what was expected.

But I couldn't. Not yet. Not while the doubt gnawed at my heart, the fear that Bastian's words might be true, that I might already be carrying his child.

"I need to go," I said suddenly, the words escaping before I could stop them. "I... I need some air."

My mother looked surprised, but she nodded, her concern evident. "Of course, dear. Take your time. We'll be here when you're ready to talk."

I didn't wait for further permission. I fled the room, the oppressive atmosphere suffocating me as I made my way outside. The fresh air hit me like a wave, but it did little to clear my mind, the tangled mess of thoughts and fears only growing more chaotic.

What was I to do? How could I possibly make this decision when the consequences were so dire? Every path seemed to lead to ruin, and I was trapped, caught in a web of my own making.

The wind rustled the leaves in the garden, but I barely noticed. My hands trembled as I wrapped my arms around myself, the weight of my future pressing down on me like a vice.

Could I truly marry Bastian? Could I face him every day, knowing the fear he had instilled in me, the way he had used my own doubts against me?

And what if I refused? Could I live with the consequences of that choice, the scandal that would follow if my worst fears were realized?

The questions circled endlessly in my mind, each one more terrifying than the last. But there were no answers, no easy solutions. I was alone, trapped in a nightmare of my own making, with no escape in sight.

I didn't know how long I stood there, lost in thought, but eventually, the sound of footsteps brought me back to reality. Anne was approaching, her expression concerned as she reached out to touch my arm.

"Adelaide," she said softly, her voice full of worry. "Are you all right?"

I looked at her, my eyes filled with the fear and uncertainty that had taken hold of me. "Anne... what am I going to do?"

She hesitated, her brow furrowing as she searched for the right words. "Whatever you decide, Adelaide, you have to do what's right for you. This is your life, your future. No one else can make this choice for you."

Her words were kind, but they did little to ease the turmoil in my heart. How could I possibly know what was right when every option seemed wrong?

But as I looked into Anne's eyes, I realized that she was right. This was my decision, and mine alone. I couldn't let my family's expectations, Bastian's threats, or even my own fears dictate my future.

I had to find the strength to make this choice, whatever it might be. And I had to do it soon.

"I need time," I whispered, more to myself than to Anne.

"Then take it," Anne replied, her voice gentle but firm. "But don't let anyone else decide for you. This is your life, Adelaide. Make sure it's the one you want to live."

I nodded, the weight of her words settling over me like a heavy blanket. I didn't know what I was going to do, but I knew that I had to make this decision on my own terms, whatever the consequences might be.

17

A Humorous Interlude

The tension at home had become unbearable, the weight of my family's expectations pressing down on me like a suffocating blanket. I needed to escape, to breathe, to find some semblance of normalcy amid the chaos that had taken over my life. So, when Anne suggested that I attend the local fair with a few of my suitors, I agreed, hoping the lighthearted atmosphere might offer some relief from the relentless pressure that had consumed me.

The fair was a riot of color and noise, the air filled with the scents of roasted chestnuts and sweet treats. Children ran about with sticky hands, their laughter echoing through the lively crowd. Booths lined the square, offering everything from games of chance to the finest ribbons and trinkets. It was the perfect distraction, and for a brief moment, I felt a small measure of peace.

I had barely arrived when Mr. Harold Davies, a particularly persistent suitor with a penchant for trying too hard, rushed over, his face flushed with excitement. "Miss Blair! How delightful to see you here! May I have the honor of escorting you?"

I forced a smile, trying to push the anxiety from my mind. "Of course, Mr. Davies."

He offered his arm, and I took it, allowing him to lead me through the bustling fairgrounds. As we walked, he chattered incessantly about the latest trends in fashion, the quality of his family's estate, and anything else that came to mind. His attempts to impress were both endearing and exhausting, and I found myself struggling to keep up with his enthusiasm.

But despite his best efforts, the outing proved to be an amusing diversion. At one point, Mr. Davies insisted on trying his hand at a game of ring toss, only to have the rings bounce off the pegs and land in the mud. He sputtered in frustration, and I couldn't help but laugh at his misfortune, much to his chagrin.

Not long after, another suitor, Lord William, a well-meaning but clumsy young man, tried his hand at winning me a stuffed bear at the shooting gallery. He missed every single target, and I found myself biting back laughter as he blushed furiously, offering me the consolation prize of a wilted flower instead.

It was all good-natured fun, and for a while, I managed to forget the heavy burdens weighing on my mind. I even allowed myself to enjoy a particularly delicious slice of cake, convincing myself that a little indulgence wouldn't hurt. After all, it wasn't every day that I had the chance to escape the pressures of life and simply be a young woman at a fair, surrounded by admirers and the thrill of harmless flirtation.

As the afternoon wore on, we found ourselves at a booth selling brightly colored balloons. Mr. Davies, ever the showman, insisted on purchasing a bouquet of them for me, despite my protests. I accepted them with a gracious smile, secretly wondering how on earth I was going to manage holding onto them all.

Just as I was beginning to enjoy myself, a hush fell over the crowd, and I felt a chill run down my spine. The hairs on the back of my neck stood on end, and I knew, without turning around, who had just arrived.

"Miss Blair," came the familiar, low voice of Duke Bastian.

I turned slowly, the sight of him sending a jolt of anxiety through my chest. He stood a few paces away, his dark, commanding presence cutting through the lively atmosphere of the fair like a blade. The crowd parted around him, as if the very air had shifted in deference to his arrival.

The suitors who had been so eager to impress me moments before suddenly found other things to do, retreating like nervous schoolboys. Even Mr. Davies, who had been full of bravado just seconds ago, made a hasty excuse and hurried off, leaving me standing there with a fistful of balloons and a sinking feeling in my stomach.

"Your Grace," I said, trying to maintain some semblance of composure. "I didn't expect to see you here."

Bastian's gaze swept over the fairgrounds, his expression one of thinly veiled disdain. "Clearly."

The lighthearted mood of the fair evaporated in an instant, replaced by a tension so thick I could scarcely breathe. Bastian's eyes narrowed as they locked onto mine, and I knew immediately that whatever had brought him here, it was not good.

"May I have a word with you, Miss Blair?" he asked, though it was not so much a question as a command.

I hesitated, my mind racing. The last thing I wanted was to be alone with him, especially here, in the middle of the fair. But I also knew that refusing him outright would only draw more attention, and the last thing I needed was another scandal on my hands.

Reluctantly, I nodded. "Of course, Your Grace."

Bastian reached out, his hand brushing against my arm as he led me away from the crowd, his grip firm and unyielding. The festive sounds of the fair faded into the background as we walked, the noise and color of the afternoon seeming distant and irrelevant now that he was here.

We stopped near a small grove of trees, the shade offering a modicum of privacy from the bustling fairgrounds. Bastian turned to face me, his expression cold and unforgiving.

"What do you think you're doing?" he asked, his voice laced with irritation.

I blinked in surprise. "What do you mean?"

"You're parading yourself around with these... these suitors, as if nothing has happened. As if you haven't already made a commitment."

I felt a surge of anger at his words. "I have made no such commitment, Your Grace. I agreed to consider your proposal, nothing more."

Bastian's eyes darkened, his patience clearly wearing thin. "You know what I'm referring to, Adelaide. This charade—playing the part of a carefree debutante while you carry my child—it's not only foolish, it's dangerous."

My breath caught in my throat, the reality of his words crashing over me like a tidal wave. "I'm not even sure if I'm pregnant," I snapped, folding my arms across my chest in defiance. "So there's no need for you to be so sure of yourself and set me straight."

Bastian's gaze was unrelenting, his expression hard as stone. "Whether or not you're certain, I am. And until we know for sure, I will act as if you are."

His hand moved then, the tip of his index finger brushing lightly against my stomach. The touch was barely there, but it was enough to send a shiver of fear through me. "As long as there is even the possibility that you are carrying my child, I have every right to be concerned about your actions."

I stared at him, my anger flaring once more. "You have no right to dictate my life, Your Grace. We're nothing to each other—nobodies."

His expression didn't waver, but there was something in his eyes that made my blood run cold. "As long as the child remains in your womb, you and I are bound, Adelaide. Whether you like it or not."

The words hung between us, heavy and suffocating. I felt a wave of nausea rise within me, but this time it wasn't the fear of pregnancy that caused it. It was the realization that Bastian was right. If I was pregnant, I would be tied to him forever, whether I wanted to be or not.

But I wasn't ready to give in, not yet. I straightened my shoulders, forcing myself to meet his gaze. "You're assuming too much, Your Grace. I may not even be pregnant."

"Perhaps," he said quietly, his voice low and dangerous. "But until we know for certain, you should be more careful with your actions. It's early yet, Adelaide. You wouldn't want to do anything that might jeopardize the child's health."

His words hit me like a slap in the face, the implication clear. I felt my hands curl into fists, my anger boiling over. "You think you can control me, frighten me into submission with your threats and your arrogance. But I won't let you, Your Grace. I won't."

Without waiting for a response, I turned on my heel and walked away, leaving him standing there in the shade of the trees. The balloons I had been holding drifted up into the sky as I released them, the colorful orbs floating away like the last remnants of the carefree day I had hoped to enjoy.

But as I walked back toward the fair, my heart heavy with anger and fear, I knew that there was no escaping the reality of my situation. Bastian had made it clear that he wasn't going to let this go, and no matter how much I tried to deny it, the possibility of pregnancy loomed over me like a dark cloud.

I didn't look back at him, but I could feel his gaze on me as I walked away, the weight of his presence pressing down on me with every step.

18

The Duke's Persistence

The days that followed my encounter with Bastian at the fair were a strange mix of tension and uncertainty. I tried to return to my daily routines, to lose myself in the familiar rhythms of life at Windermere Manor, but it was impossible to escape the shadow that Bastian had cast over me. His words, his presence, his unrelenting confidence—it all weighed heavily on my mind, leaving me feeling trapped and powerless.

And then, to my surprise, Bastian began to court me. Not in the traditional sense, with flowers and poetry, but in his own unconventional way—one that left me constantly on edge, unsure of his intentions.

It started with small gestures, things that were almost imperceptible but impossible to ignore. A bouquet of lilies, my favorite flowers, arrived one morning without a note. A book I had mentioned in passing was delivered to my door the next day. And then there were the letters—short, concise notes that were direct and to the point. He never mentioned the proposal, never asked for an answer, but his words always carried an undercurrent of expectation, a reminder that he was waiting.

But it wasn't just the gifts or the letters that unsettled me. It was the way Bastian seemed to genuinely care for the well-being of the child he believed I was carrying. He sent word to the manor asking about my health, my diet, whether I was getting enough rest. His concern was unnerving, not because it was unwelcome, but because it was so at odds with the cold, calculating man

I had come to know.

I found myself torn between anger and confusion. Bastian's persistence was infuriating, yet there was a part of me that couldn't help but be touched by his concern. It was as if he was trying to show me a side of himself that I had never seen before—a side that was soft, even vulnerable. But I couldn't trust it. I couldn't trust him.

Then came the invitation.

It arrived one morning, delivered by a footman with impeccable timing. The envelope was heavy, the paper embossed with the crest of the Duchess of Abernathy—a woman known for her influence in society and her ability to make or break reputations with a single word. The invitation was for an exclusive garden party, a gathering of the most elite members of society. It was the kind of event where connections were forged, alliances were made, and fortunes were determined.

I stared at the invitation, my mind racing. Attending this party could be my chance to secure a proposal from one of the many eligible men who would undoubtedly be in attendance. If I could find a suitable husband quickly, I could put an end to this nightmare, and Bastian's hold over me would be broken.

But the thought of being recognized, of someone whispering behind their fan about the rumors that had begun to swirl around me, filled me with dread. Still, I knew I couldn't afford to miss this opportunity. I had to take the risk.

With a resolve born of desperation, I decided to attend.

The day of the garden party dawned bright and clear, the air filled with the scent of blooming flowers and the promise of summer. I dressed with care, choosing a gown of pale blue silk that complimented my complexion and wore my hair in a simple but elegant style. If I was to make an impression, I would need to present myself as the picture of calm and confidence, even if I was anything but.

As I arrived at the Duchess's estate, I was struck by the sheer opulence of the setting. The gardens were vast, filled with carefully tended flowers and towering hedges that created a sense of privacy and intimacy. Guests milled about, their laughter and conversation filling the air as they sipped champagne and nibbled on delicate pastries.

I took a deep breath, steeling myself for the task ahead. This was my chance—my chance to find a husband and secure my future. I couldn't let fear hold me back.

But as I made my way through the gardens, exchanging pleasantries with those I passed, I couldn't shake the feeling that I was being watched. It wasn't until I turned a corner and found myself face to face with Duke Bastian that I realized why.

He was there, of course. I should have known he would be. The Duke of Lightwood was never one to miss an opportunity to make his presence known, especially when it came to me.

"Miss Blair," he greeted me, his voice smooth and composed, as if our last encounter had never happened. "You look lovely today."

I forced a smile, my heart racing. "Your Grace. I didn't expect to see you here."

Bastian's eyes glinted with something unreadable. "Did you think I would let you out of my sight for long?"

There was something in his tone that made me bristle, but I kept my composure. "I'm here to enjoy the garden party, Your Grace. Nothing more."

"Of course," he said, though his gaze never left mine. "And how are you feeling?"

The question was loaded, and we both knew it. I swallowed hard, trying to keep my voice steady. "I'm fine, thank you."

"Good," he replied, his tone deceptively casual. "I would hate for anything to spoil your day."

Before I could respond, the Duchess of Abernathy approached, her eyes twinkling with mischief. "Ah, Miss Blair! And the Duke of Lightwood. What a delightful surprise to see the two of you together."

I opened my mouth to respond, but before I could, Bastian spoke. "Indeed, Your Grace. In fact, there's something I've been meaning to discuss with Miss Blair for some time."

My heart skipped a beat, dread pooling in the pit of my stomach. Whatever Bastian was planning, I knew it couldn't be good.

The Duchess raised an eyebrow, clearly intrigued. "Oh? Do tell, Duke Bastian."

Bastian turned to face the gathered crowd, his voice carrying with the authority of a man who was used to commanding attention. "Ladies and gentlemen, I apologize for the interruption, but I have an announcement to make."

The crowd fell silent, all eyes turning toward us. My pulse quickened, panic rising in my chest. This couldn't be happening. Not here, not now.

"I have had the pleasure of knowing Miss Blair for some time now," Bastian continued, his voice calm and measured. "And it is with great honor and respect that I ask her to be my wife."

A collective gasp echoed through the garden, the air thick with anticipation. My mind went blank, the world spinning around me as I tried to process what was happening. Bastian had just proposed—publicly, in front of the most influential members of society.

I opened my mouth to protest, to refuse, but the words wouldn't come. My gaze flicked to the faces of the crowd, their expressions a mixture of shock and delight. If I refused him here, the scandal would be unimaginable. But if I accepted... I would be sealing my fate.

Bastian turned to me, his eyes locking onto mine with an intensity that left me breathless. "Adelaide," he said softly, so only I could hear. "You don't have to decide right now. But think carefully before you refuse. This is your chance to secure your future—and the future of our child."

His words hit me like a punch to the gut. He had done it. He had manipulated the situation so that I had little choice but to accept. To refuse would be to invite scandal, to destroy any chance I had of finding another suitor. And to accept... would be to tie myself to him forever.

The garden seemed to close in around me, the eyes of the crowd like a thousand weights pressing down on my shoulders. My mind raced, but there was no escape, no way out of the trap he had set.

Bastian's hand reached out, gently taking mine. His touch was firm, but not forceful, as if he were offering me a lifeline instead of binding me to him. "Will you do me the honor of becoming my wife?"

I swallowed hard, the taste of fear bitter in my mouth. I had been so determined to resist him, to find another way, but now... what choice did I have?

With a deep breath, I nodded, the weight of the decision pressing down on me like a thousand stones. "Yes, Your Grace. I will marry you."

The crowd erupted into applause, their cheers ringing in my ears as Bastian's hand tightened around mine. But even as I smiled and curtsied, playing the part of the dutiful fiancée, I couldn't shake the feeling of dread that settled over me.

Bastian had won. He had outmaneuvered me at every turn, and now, I was his. But as I looked up at him, his eyes filled with satisfaction, I made a silent vow to myself.

I may have accepted his proposal, but I would not let him control me. Not completely. Not ever.

This was not the end. It was only the beginning.

19

The Secrets and Sentiments

The days that followed my encounter with Bastian at the fair were a strange mix of tension and uncertainty. I tried to return to my daily routines, to lose myself in the familiar rhythms of life at Windermere Manor, but it was impossible to escape the shadow that Bastian had cast over me. His words, his presence, his unrelenting confidence—it all weighed heavily on my mind, leaving me feeling trapped and powerless.

Each day, I found myself waiting for the other shoe to drop, wondering when he would make his next move. His sudden interest in my well-being was perplexing, unsettling even. I was used to seeing him as a cold, calculating man, yet his concern for me—and for the child he believed I was carrying—seemed genuine. But could it be? Could a man like Bastian truly care for anyone other than himself?

These thoughts plagued me as I wandered the corridors of Windermere, my mind restless and my heart conflicted. I found solace in my usual haunts—the library, where I lost myself in the pages of novels and poetry, and the gardens, where the scent of roses and the gentle rustle of leaves in the breeze offered a fleeting sense of peace. But even there, I couldn't escape the questions that swirled in my mind.

One afternoon, as I sat beneath the shade of the ancient oak tree that stood at the edge of the estate, I was startled by the arrival of a visitor. It was Mrs. Pritchard, the housekeeper, a woman of few words but with a gaze that missed nothing.

"Miss Blair," she began, her tone formal yet tinged with something akin to concern, "there is a matter I believe you should be aware of."

I looked up from my book, my heart quickening. "What is it, Mrs. Pritchard?"

She hesitated, her hands wringing together in an uncharacteristic display of anxiety. "It's... His Grace, the Duke of Lightwood. He has sent word that he wishes to visit Windermere in the coming days."

My breath caught in my throat. "Duke Bastian is coming here?"

"Yes, Miss," she confirmed, her eyes narrowing as she studied my reaction. "He insists that it is merely a social call, but I thought it best to inform you so that you might be prepared."

Prepared. How could I ever be prepared for Bastian? The very thought of him in my home, invading my sanctuary, made my skin crawl. But there was no avoiding it. He had made up his mind, and when Bastian Lightwood set his sights on something—or someone—there was little that could dissuade him.

"Thank you, Mrs. Pritchard," I said, forcing a smile that felt as fragile as glass. "I appreciate the warning."

She nodded, her expression softening. "If there's anything you need, Miss, you have only to ask."

As she left, I sat there in silence, the weight of Bastian's impending visit pressing down on me like a leaden cloak. What did he hope to gain by coming here? Was it another attempt to unsettle me, to remind me of the power he held over my life? Or was there something more, something deeper that I couldn't yet fathom?

The next few days passed in a blur of anxious anticipation. I found myself jumping at every sound, every knock at the door, half-expecting Bastian to appear at any moment. But he didn't. Instead, he sent more letters—short, polite notes that offered no insight into his true intentions but kept him firmly in my thoughts.

I couldn't help but feel that he was toying with me, testing my resolve, waiting for me to crack under the pressure. But I refused to give him that satisfaction. If he wanted to play games, I would meet him move for move.

It wasn't until three days later that Bastian finally arrived at Windermere. The sky was overcast, the air heavy with the promise of rain, as his carriage pulled up to the front of the manor. I watched from my window as he stepped out, his tall frame and commanding presence impossible to ignore. Even from a distance, I could see the determination in his stride, the set of his jaw.

I took a deep breath, steeling myself for what was to come. I would not be intimidated. I would face him with the same poise and resolve that I had shown him at the fair. But as I descended the stairs and made my way to the drawing-room, a new thought occurred to me—a thought that sent a chill down my spine.

What if this was more than just a visit? What if Bastian had come to force my hand, to push me into accepting his proposal once and for all? The idea seemed absurd, yet I couldn't shake the feeling that he was playing a longer game, one that I had yet to fully understand.

When I entered the drawing-room, Bastian was already there, standing by the window with his back to me. He turned as I approached, his expression unreadable, his eyes dark and intense.

"Miss Blair," he greeted me, his voice smooth as silk. "Thank you for receiving me."

"Your Grace," I replied, my own voice steady despite the turmoil in my chest. "What brings you to Windermere?"

He smiled—a slow, calculating smile that sent a shiver down my spine. "I wished to see you, of course. And to discuss a matter of some importance."

My heart skipped a beat. "And what matter would that be?"

Bastian took a step closer, his gaze locking onto mine. "Our future, Miss Blair. It's time we discussed it in earnest."

Bastian's words hung in the air between us, heavy and foreboding. My heart pounded in my chest as I searched his face for any hint of vulnerability, any sign that this was more than just another calculated move in his relentless pursuit. But all I saw was that same unyielding determination, the same steely resolve that had become all too familiar.

"Our future?" I echoed, struggling to keep my voice from trembling. "Your Grace, I'm not sure what you expect to gain from this... discussion."

Bastian's smile didn't waver, but there was a new intensity in his eyes, a sharpness that made my pulse quicken. "Adelaide," he said, his voice softening slightly, "you must know by now that I am not a man who takes no for an answer lightly. But I'm willing to hear you out—if only to understand what it is that you truly want."

What I truly want. The words echoed in my mind, mocking me. What I wanted was simple: freedom from the suffocating grip of Bastian's machinations, a chance to reclaim the life I had before he had appeared like a storm cloud on the horizon. But could I say that to him? Would he even listen?

I drew in a shaky breath, summoning every ounce of courage I had. "What I want, Your Grace, is to live my life on my own terms. To make my own choices, free from the influence of others. I cannot—will not—allow myself to be manipulated into a marriage I do not desire."

For the first time since his arrival, Bastian's smile faltered, his brow furrowing ever so slightly. "Manipulated?" he repeated, a flicker of something—surprise?—in his eyes. "Is that truly how you see it?"

"How else could I see it?" I shot back, the words spilling out before I could stop them. "You've cornered me at every turn, forced me into a position where I have no choice but to consider your proposal. And now you stand here, expecting me to simply... submit? To give in to your will because it's what you want?"

Bastian's expression hardened, his jaw tightening. "I've only ever sought to secure our future—to protect you, Adelaide. The child you carry—"

"There is no child," I interrupted, my voice firm and unyielding. The lie I had let him believe for so long had become a chain around my neck, and I was done with it. "There is no child, Your Grace. I am not pregnant, and I never was."

A tense silence fell between us, but instead of the expected shock, Bastian's eyes narrowed, his expression skeptical. "Adelaide, do not play games with me. I know the symptoms; I've seen how you've been. There's no need to deny it to spite me."

The conviction in his tone was maddening, as if he could will it to be true simply because he wanted it so. My frustration bubbled over. "I'm not playing games! The only one deluding themselves here is you. I am not pregnant, and I have no intention of pretending otherwise just to placate your ego."

He took a step closer, his presence overwhelming, his eyes boring into mine as if trying to peel away the layers of my resolve. "You've been ill, fainting even. The timing is too precise to be coincidence. You expect me to believe that all of that was for naught?"

"Yes," I insisted, my voice rising with each word. "Yes, I do. What you've been observing is nothing more than exhaustion, stress—brought on by *you*, if you must know. But it is not—will never be—proof of a child."

Bastian's jaw clenched, a flicker of doubt crossing his features, but it was quickly smothered by his stubborn resolve. "So you say now, but I know what I saw."

I wanted to scream, to shake him, to force him to see the truth that he refused to acknowledge. But instead, I took a deep breath, forcing myself to stay calm. "You see what you want to see. And that's the problem. You've convinced yourself that you know what's best for me, for us, without ever considering what I want."

Bastian's eyes flared with frustration, but he held his tongue. For a moment, I thought I might have reached him, that he might actually listen. But then his expression hardened again, his gaze turning cold and calculating.

"You've played your hand well, Miss Blair," he said quietly, his voice devoid of the charm and confidence it usually carried. "I'll give you that. But do not think for a moment that this changes anything."

A cold shiver ran down my spine. "What do you mean?"

"I mean," he said, his voice like steel, "that I will not be so easily dismissed. You may refuse me now, but mark my words, Adelaide—I will not give up on what I want. Not ever."

I swallowed hard, forcing myself to meet his gaze head-on. "And what is it that you want, Your Grace? Is it truly me, or just the idea of possessing something you cannot have?"

For a long moment, he said nothing, his eyes boring into mine with an intensity that made my skin prickle. When he finally spoke, his voice was low and dangerous. "Make no mistake, Adelaide. I want you. But more than that,

I want you to want me."

I felt a pang of fear, but I refused to let it show. "Then you'll be waiting a long time, Your Grace. Because I will not be won over by threats or manipulation."

Bastian's lips curved into a tight, humorless smile. "We'll see about that."

Without another word, he turned on his heel and strode toward the door, leaving me standing there, my heart pounding in my chest. The moment he was gone, the tension that had coiled in my body like a spring finally released, and I sank into the nearest chair, my hands trembling.

I had done it. I had refused him. But as I sat there, trying to catch my breath, I couldn't shake the feeling that this was far from over. Bastian Lightwood was not a man who took rejection lightly. I had won this round, but the battle was just beginning.

As I stared out the window, watching the dark clouds gather on the horizon, I knew that I would have to be more vigilant than ever. Bastian's threats weren't empty, and I had no doubt that he would find new ways to try and bend me to his will. But I had made a vow to myself, and I would not be swayed.

This was my life, my future. And I would fight for it with everything I had.

20

The Unwanted Epiphany

The aftermath of Bastian's visit left me feeling more rattled than I cared to admit. His persistence, his unyielding certainty, had shaken something loose in me. I had prided myself on my ability to keep him at arm's length, to resist his manipulations, but the doubt he had planted in my mind was like a thorn I couldn't dislodge.

Days passed, and with each one, my unease grew. I hadn't yet menstruated, and my monthly cycle was more than three weeks late. I had dismissed it at first, attributing it to the stress of dealing with Bastian and the upheaval in my life. But as the days turned into weeks, I could no longer ignore the gnawing fear that Bastian might be right. What if... what if there really was a child?

The thought made my stomach churn with dread. A child would change everything, would bind me to Bastian in a way that was both terrifying and irrevocable. But what if it was true? What if the very thing I had denied with such certainty was, in fact, a reality?

I couldn't bear to stay cooped up in Windermere with my thoughts any longer. I needed air, space to think, to sort through the chaos in my mind. Without much thought, I threw on my cloak and set out for the city, hoping that the bustle of London might offer some distraction, some clarity.

As I walked through the crowded streets, my mind swirled with conflicting emotions. I was angry—angry at Bastian for his relentless pursuit, angry at myself for even entertaining the possibility that he might be right. How dare he force this on me, make me question my own body, my own reality?

But as I turned down a quieter street, my steps faltering slightly, a wave of dizziness washed over me. The ground seemed to tilt beneath my feet, and I reached out to steady myself against a nearby wall, my breath coming in shallow gasps. Panic gripped me as I fought to regain control, my vision swimming with dark spots.

It was as if the world had suddenly closed in around me, the bustling city fading into the background as my body betrayed me. My hand instinctively went to my abdomen, a cold realization creeping into my mind. This wasn't just stress. This was something more, something I couldn't explain away.

Before I could fully comprehend what was happening, I heard a familiar voice—one that sent a jolt of both relief and frustration through me.

"Adelaide!"

I turned, still leaning against the wall, and found myself face to face with Bastian. His expression was a mixture of concern and something else, something almost like triumph. He crossed the distance between us in a few long strides, his hand reaching out to steady me.

"What's wrong? You look pale," he said, his voice low and urgent.

"I—I'm fine," I managed to stammer, though the words felt hollow even to me. "I just need a moment."

But Bastian wasn't convinced. His eyes narrowed as he studied my face, his hand still resting on my arm. "You're not fine. Something's wrong."

I wanted to push him away, to deny everything, but the truth was, I didn't know what was happening to me. And that terrified me more than anything.

"Please," I whispered, my voice trembling, "help me."

Something shifted in Bastian's expression—an almost imperceptible softening of his features, a flash of vulnerability that I had never seen before. Without another word, he slipped his arm around my waist, supporting my weight as he guided me through the streets.

We walked in silence, the noise of the city fading into the background as I focused on putting one foot in front of the other. I didn't know where Bastian was taking me, and I didn't care. All I knew was that I couldn't do this alone.

Eventually, we arrived at a narrow alleyway, the kind of place I would never have ventured on my own. Bastian led me to a small, nondescript door tucked away between two dilapidated buildings. He knocked twice, and after a moment, the door creaked open, revealing an elderly man with wild white hair and a pair of spectacles perched precariously on the end of his nose.

"What is it?" the man grumbled, squinting at us through his spectacles.

Bastian didn't miss a beat. "This young lady needs to be examined. She's been feeling unwell."

The old man—clearly a doctor, though not of the most reputable sort—peered at me, his gaze sharp and assessing. "Come in, then. I'll have a look."

The room we entered was small and cramped, filled with an odd assortment of medical instruments and books stacked haphazardly on every available surface. The air was thick with the smell of herbs and something else I couldn't quite place—something slightly sour and metallic.

Bastian helped me into a chair, his hand lingering on my shoulder as the doctor shuffled over to me, his movements slow but deliberate. He examined me with a practiced eye, asking a few terse questions before instructing me to lie back on a rickety examination table that looked as if it had seen better days.

I followed his instructions, my heart pounding in my chest as the reality of the situation began to sink in. I was about to find out if my worst fear was true—if I was carrying Bastian's child.

The doctor's examination was quick and efficient, his hands moving with a confidence that belied his shabby appearance. When he finally stepped back, his expression was unreadable.

"Well?" Bastian asked, his voice tight with tension. "What's the verdict?"

The doctor glanced between the two of us, his eyes lingering on Bastian for a moment before he spoke. "It's too early to say for certain, but it's likely that the young lady is indeed with child. However, I'd advise waiting a few more weeks before drawing any final conclusions."

A cold shiver ran down my spine, my worst fears seemingly confirmed. I felt Bastian's hand tighten on my shoulder, his grip firm but not painful. There was a moment of heavy silence, and in that moment, something in me broke.

I had fought so hard to resist him, to deny the possibility, but now... what was left? If I truly was pregnant, then everything would change. My life, my future—it would all be tied to Bastian in a way I could never escape.

I sat up slowly, my mind racing. Bastian's presence beside me was both a comfort and a torment, a reminder of the power he held over me. But as I looked up at him, his eyes filled with an intensity that sent a shiver down my spine, I knew that I couldn't fight him anymore. Not like this.

"Bastian," I said quietly, my voice barely above a whisper. "If this is true... if I am pregnant, then I have no choice but to accept what's happening. But I want you to understand something."

His gaze softened slightly, as if sensing the change in me. "What is it?"

I swallowed hard, meeting his gaze head-on. "I may accept your presence in my life, but that doesn't mean I've given up. I will protect this child—our child—if it comes to that. But I will do so on my terms. I will not be your possession. I will not be controlled."

For a moment, he said nothing, his eyes searching mine as if trying to decipher my true feelings. Then, slowly, he nodded. "I understand, Adelaide. But know this—I will do whatever it takes to protect you and our child. Whatever it takes."

His words sent a chill down my spine, but there was also a strange sense of relief in them—a relief that, for now at least, I wasn't alone in this. Even if I didn't fully trust Bastian, even if I couldn't bring myself to like him, I knew that he was determined to see this through.

As we left the doctor's cramped office, the reality of what might be ahead settled over me like a heavy cloak. My life had changed irrevocably, and there was no turning back. But as Bastian's hand rested lightly on the small of my back, guiding me through the bustling streets of London, I made a silent vow to myself.

I would survive this. I would protect my future, and if there was a child, I would protect them too. But I would do it my way. Even if that meant accepting Bastian's presence in my life, I would never let him control me completely. Not ever.

21

A Growing Affection

The days that followed Bastian's public proposal and our encounter in a narrow alley were a whirlwind of activity and emotion. The shock of accepting his offer, of being thrust into the role of the future Duchess of Lightwood and the possibility of me actually being pregnant, left me reeling. But even as I tried to come to terms with what had happened, I found myself spending more time with Bastian than I ever had before.

To my surprise, the cold, distant Duke I had once feared began to reveal a side of himself that I hadn't expected. It was subtle at first—small gestures, moments of quiet concern that caught me off guard. I had been prepared for a marriage of convenience, a union built on duty and obligation, but what I found instead was something far more complex.

One crisp afternoon, we were walking through the gardens of his estate, the leaves rustling in the breeze as autumn began to take hold. The air was cool, and I had brought a shawl to ward off the chill, but Bastian seemed unusually attentive to my comfort.

"Are you warm enough, Adelaide?" he asked, his voice laced with genuine concern. "Too much exposure to the wind isn't good for pregnant women."

I opened my mouth to protest, to remind him that I wasn't even certain I was pregnant, but the look in his eyes stopped me. He was serious—genuinely worried about my well-being. For a moment, the Duke's usual stern demeanor softened, and I saw something else in his expression—something protective and tender.

He reached out, adjusting the shawl around my shoulders with a gentleness that took me by surprise. "There, that's better," he murmured, his hand lingering on my arm for just a moment longer than necessary.

I wanted to protest, to tell him that his concern was unnecessary, but the words caught in my throat. Seeing him like this, so focused on my comfort, made it difficult to argue. Instead, I found myself nodding, a small smile tugging at the corners of my lips.

"Thank you," I said quietly, my heart fluttering in a way that it hadn't before.

As we continued our walk, Bastian kept a close eye on me, ensuring that the path was clear and that the wind didn't pick up too much. It was a side of him I hadn't seen before—a side that was attentive, even caring.

When it was time to return to the manor, Bastian insisted that we take the carriage, despite the short distance. And it wasn't just when we were outside. Whenever we traveled in a carriage, Bastian would insist on the horses moving at a snail's pace, far slower than was necessary. "We must be careful," he would say, his hand resting protectively on my arm. "A bumpy ride could be dangerous for the baby."

I glanced at him, my heart skipping a beat. "Bastian, I'm not even certain that I'm—"

He cut me off with a gentle smile, one that reached his eyes and made it impossible for me to continue. "I know, Adelaide. But until we're sure, I want to be cautious. I won't take any chances."

I wanted to roll my eyes, to tell him he was being ridiculous, but the way he looked at me, the sincerity in his gaze, left me speechless. He seemed so earnest, so genuinely worried about my comfort, that I couldn't bring myself to protest. I could only nod, my thoughts swirling in confusion and something else—something I couldn't quite name.

As the carriage began to move, Bastian's hand found mine, his touch warm and reassuring. We rode in silence, the gentle sway of the carriage and the rhythmic clip-clop of the horses' hooves creating a soothing backdrop. Despite my initial reservations, I found myself relaxing, the tension that had gripped me since his proposal slowly beginning to ease.

One afternoon, as we rode together in his carriage, the sunlight filtering through the trees and casting dappled shadows on the road, Bastian leaned closer to me, his expression thoughtful. "Adelaide," he began, his voice low, "you haven't had your period yet, have you?"

The question caught me off guard, and I felt a flush of embarrassment rise to my cheeks. It was such a personal thing to ask, and yet there was no malice in his tone, only quiet concern.

"I... no, I haven't," I admitted, my voice barely above a whisper.

Bastian nodded, his eyes darkening with something I couldn't quite place. "Then it's possible, isn't it? That you're carrying our child."

I opened my mouth to respond, to tell him that we couldn't be sure, that it was too soon to jump to conclusions, but the words caught in my throat. Because the truth was, I didn't know. And the more time I spent with him, the more I began to wonder if maybe, just maybe, he was right.

Could it be that I was already pregnant? The thought filled me with a strange mixture of fear and awe, and I found myself unconsciously placing a hand on my abdomen, as if I could feel some sign of life within.

Bastian noticed the gesture and smiled, his eyes softening. "You'll be a wonderful mother, Adelaide," he said, his voice filled with quiet conviction.

I felt a lump form in my throat, and for the first time, I couldn't bring myself to deny it. What if he was right? What if there really was a child growing inside me, a child that was ours?

Bastian reached out and gently placed his hand on my stomach. The touch was light, almost reverent, and it sent a shiver down my spine.

"Your belly will grow soon," he said quietly, his eyes locked on mine. "It won't be long before it's too big to hide under a wedding dress. We should move quickly, Adelaide."

His words hung in the air, heavy with unspoken meaning. I could feel the warmth of his hand through the fabric of my dress, the weight of his touch grounding me in a way that was both comforting and terrifying. It was as if, in that moment, he was claiming not just me, but the life that might be growing within me.

I wanted to protest, to tell him that we were rushing into things, that we should wait and see what happened. But when I looked into his eyes, saw the way he gazed at me with such tenderness, the words failed me. There was something about the way he spoke of our child—of *our* future—that left me speechless. He also determined to ensure that we would be married before any rumors could spread—or before my belly grew too large to hide.

Maybe it was the way he was so certain, so unwavering in his belief that I was already carrying his child. Maybe it was the way he touched me, not with the cool detachment of a man fulfilling a duty, but with the warmth and protectiveness of a father. Whatever it was, it left me feeling more confused than ever, and I could only nod in response, my heart too full of conflicting emotions to speak.

As the carriage rolled on, I leaned back against the cushioned seat, my mind racing. Bastian was planning everything, moving forward as if the future were already decided. And maybe it was. Maybe, despite all my doubts and fears, I was truly beginning to believe that I was pregnant, that I was carrying his child.

But as I sat there, Bastian's hand resting gently on my stomach, I knew one thing for certain: I was no longer the same woman I had been before. Something had changed, shifted within me, and I couldn't deny the growing affection I felt for the man beside me.

I had spent so long fearing him, resenting him, but now... now I saw him in a different light. He was still the Duke of Lightwood, still cold and calculating in many ways, but there was also a warmth there, a deep well of care and protectiveness that I hadn't seen before.

And it was that warmth, that tenderness, that made me wonder if maybe— just maybe—I could learn to care for him too.

The thought was terrifying, but also strangely comforting. Because if I was going to marry him, if I was going to carry his child, then perhaps it was better to do so with a heart that was not filled with fear and resentment, but with something more... something softer, something that could grow into love.

22

The Duke's Baby Fever

E ver since I became convinced that Adelaide was pregnant, my life had taken on a singular focus—preparing for our future child. I had never imagined myself as the paternal type, but now, I found myself deeply invested in every aspect of our future, from the smallest details of the nursery to the exact shade of blue for the baby's first set of blankets.

"Your Grace," Alfred, my ever-practical butler, had reminded me several times, "Miss Blair's pregnancy has not been confirmed."

"Yes, Alfred, I'm aware," I replied, dismissing his concerns with a wave of my hand. "But I am quite certain."

Alfred, bless his long-suffering soul, merely raised an eyebrow. "And how can you be so certain, Your Grace?"

I looked up from the plans I had been reviewing for the nursery—elegantly appointed, naturally, with the finest furnishings that money could buy—and fixed Alfred with what I hoped was a reassuring smile. "She hasn't had her period, Alfred. That's confirmation enough for me."

"Very well, Your Grace," Alfred replied, though I could hear the skepticism in his voice. "But perhaps it would be wise to wait for more... definitive proof before proceeding with such enthusiasm."

"Enthusiasm?" I echoed, feigning ignorance as I glanced at the collection of baby items I had ordered to be delivered to Lightwood Manor. The finest crib, a selection of soft, handcrafted toys, and enough baby clothes to outfit a small army of infants. "I'm merely being prepared."

Alfred's lips twitched in what I suspected was an attempt to suppress a smile. "Of course, Your Grace. Preparedness is commendable."

I turned my attention back to the nursery plans, but my mind was elsewhere—specifically, on the image of Adelaide, heavily pregnant, sitting on my lap as we spent a quiet evening together. It was a vision that had taken root in my mind, and one I found myself returning to time and time again.

In my mind's eye, I could see it clearly: Adelaide would be wearing one of those flowing maternity gowns that accentuated her growing belly, her hair cascading over her shoulders in soft waves. She would be sitting comfortably on my lap, her arms wrapped around my neck as she leaned in to kiss me, her lips soft and warm against mine. And all the while, my hand would rest protectively on her swollen belly, feeling the life growing within her.

It was a comforting thought, one that made the prospect of marriage not only bearable but desirable. I had always seen marriage as a necessity, an obligation to ensure the continuation of the Lightwood line. But now, I found myself looking forward to it—not just for the sake of the child I was certain Adelaide was carrying, but for the life we could build together.

"Your Grace," Alfred's voice interrupted my reverie, "might I suggest we slow down the preparations until Miss Blair's condition is confirmed?"

I looked at him, my brows furrowing. "Alfred, whether Adelaide is pregnant now or not, she will be eventually. The wedding must proceed regardless, and the nursery will be needed sooner or later."

Alfred inclined his head, his expression one of polite acquiescence. "As you wish, Your Grace."

With Alfred's gentle reminder lingering in the back of my mind, I resolved to continue with the preparations, albeit with a bit more discretion. The wedding was set to take place soon, and there was still much to be done. But as I reviewed the guest list, the menu, and the arrangements for the ceremony, my thoughts kept drifting back to that vision of Adelaide.

I could imagine it so vividly—coming home after a long day's work, finding her in the library or perhaps in our private sitting room, her hand resting on her belly as she read or sketched. I would take her in my arms, feeling the warmth of her body against mine, and we would share a quiet moment together. She would smile at me, that soft, genuine smile that I had come to treasure, and she would tell me about her day.

And then, as the evening drew to a close, we would retire to our chambers. Adelaide would rest her head on my shoulder as I held her close, my hand once again finding its place on her belly. We would talk about the future, about the child we were bringing into the world, and I would tell her how much she meant to me—how much they both meant to me.

The thought of it filled me with a warmth I hadn't known I was capable of. It was more than just the satisfaction of duty fulfilled; it was a genuine desire to build a life with Adelaide, to share in the joys and challenges of parenthood.

"Your Grace," Alfred's voice brought me back to the present, "shall I arrange for a visit from the midwife?"

I hesitated for a moment before nodding. "Yes, Alfred. Discreetly, of course. But it would be wise to have her examine Adelaide, just to be certain."

"Very good, Your Grace," Alfred replied, a hint of approval in his tone.

As Alfred left to make the necessary arrangements, I leaned back in my chair, allowing myself to indulge in that vision one more time. I could see it so clearly—Adelaide, with her hand on her growing belly, smiling up at me as we prepared to welcome our child into the world.

Whether or not she was pregnant at this very moment, I knew that the future I envisioned was not far off. And I would do everything in my power to ensure that it was a future filled with love, warmth, and the joy of a family we would build together.

For the first time in a long while, I felt a sense of contentment settle over me. The wedding was imminent, the preparations nearly complete, and soon enough, I would have everything I had ever wanted—everything I had never even realized I needed.

And as I closed my eyes, the vision of Adelaide and our child once again filled my thoughts, bringing with it a smile that I couldn't suppress. Whether she was pregnant now or in the future, one thing was certain: Adelaide was mine, and together, we would face whatever the future held.

23

Beneath the Willow Tree

The day of our picnic dawned with a light breeze and clear skies, a perfect backdrop for the charade Bastian and I were playing. My emotions were a tangled web of apprehension and reluctant acceptance. I had agreed to this outing, allowing Bastian to woo me in his peculiar way, but my heart was still guarded, my mind wary of what it all meant.

Bastian arrived at Windermere in a sleek carriage that drew the attention of the entire household. My mother, ever the picture of decorum, watched from the drawing-room window, her sharp eyes taking in every detail of the Duke's approach. I could almost feel her satisfaction—her daughter, courted by the Duke of Lightwood himself. But she didn't see what lay beneath the surface, the uncertainty, the fear that gnawed at me.

"Miss Blair," Bastian greeted me with a slight bow as I descended the steps, his tone warm and his gaze lingering on mine. There was a possessiveness in his eyes that made my pulse quicken—not entirely out of fear, but something else I wasn't ready to admit.

"Your Grace," I replied, my voice as even as I could manage. I was acutely aware of my family's eyes on us, particularly my mother's, as she hovered in the doorway, watching us with thinly veiled interest.

Bastian offered me his arm, and I took it, allowing him to lead me to the waiting carriage. He was all charm as he exchanged pleasantries with my mother, making her practically beam with approval. I could see how this would look to anyone on the outside—a duke courting a young lady with all the propriety expected of his rank. But I knew better. This was no ordinary courtship.

Once we were settled in the carriage, Bastian's demeanor shifted. The mask of the polished duke slipped just slightly, revealing a more tender, possessive side. He looked at me with something close to pride, his hand resting on the seat between us, fingers twitching as if he wanted to reach out but was holding himself back.

It wasn't long before he gave in to the urge, placing his hand gently on my belly. I stiffened at the unexpected intimacy, but his touch was surprisingly tender. He rubbed slow circles on my abdomen, his expression softening as he looked down at my stomach.

"Hello, little one," he murmured, his voice so low that it sent shivers down my spine. "You must be patient, darling. Soon enough, we'll all be together, your mother and I, after the wedding."

His words, spoken so casually yet with such conviction, made my heart pound in my chest. The weight of what he was saying, the certainty with which he spoke, was suffocating. I could hardly bring myself to breathe, the carriage's rhythm echoing the turmoil within me.

I couldn't bring myself to respond, my thoughts too muddled to form coherent words. All I could do was sit there, letting him speak to a child that may or may not exist, feeling the walls of my carefully constructed defenses start to crumble.

The rest of the journey passed in a tense silence, punctuated only by the clatter of the train as it sped towards our destination. When we arrived at the park, the air was crisp and fresh, the perfect contrast to the heaviness that had settled over me.

We found a spot beneath a large willow tree, its sweeping branches offering privacy and shade. Bastian spread out a blanket on the grass, his movements careful and precise, as if he were setting the stage for some grand performance. I could see how hard he was trying, how much he wanted to win me over, and despite everything, it tugged at something deep within me.

As we settled down, Bastian took great care in arranging the picnic. He handed me a glass of lemonade, watching me with those intense eyes of his. I sipped it slowly, trying to calm the flutter of nerves in my stomach.

A sudden breeze swept through the park, and a few strands of my hair escaped their pins, blowing across my face. Bastian reached out without hesitation, gently tucking the stray strands behind my ear. The simple gesture was so uncharacteristically tender that it caught me off guard, sending a warm flush through my cheeks.

"You should let it down more often," he remarked, his tone almost playful as he regarded my hair with a curious gaze. "It suits you."

I managed a small smile, unsure of how to respond. The man who had manipulated me, who had forced me into a corner, was now looking at me as if I were something precious. It was disarming, confusing.

We talked about inconsequential things—about the weather, the beauty of the park, the upcoming social events. But there was a tension beneath our words, a tension that neither of us acknowledged but both felt keenly. Bastian's hand found its way to my belly again, his touch lingering as if to remind me of the life he believed we had created together.

And then, without warning, he lifted me onto his lap, his arms wrapping around me protectively. The sudden closeness made my breath catch, but I didn't resist. There was something reassuring in the way he held me, as if for that moment, all his scheming and maneuvering were set aside.

His lips found mine in a kiss that was far gentler than I had expected. There was no urgency, no force—just a slow, deliberate tenderness that took me by surprise. His hand, warm and firm, rested on my stomach, as if anchoring us both to the reality of the situation. For the first time, I felt a flicker of something—something I had been resisting for so long. A thrill, a sense of warmth that I couldn't quite name.

When he finally pulled away, his lips trailed down to my belly, pressing a soft kiss there that sent another shiver through me. I could hardly believe this was the same man who had cornered me at every turn, who had left me feeling trapped and powerless. And yet, here he was, treating me with a care and consideration I hadn't expected.

"I wonder," Bastian murmured, his lips brushing against my skin as he spoke. "Will our child have your spirit, your fire? Or will they be more like me, calculating and relentless?"

His words, spoken with such raw honesty, made my breath catch in my throat. I didn't know how to answer him, didn't know how to reconcile the man before me with the one who had manipulated me so ruthlessly.

"I suppose," I whispered, my voice trembling slightly, "they'll be a mix of both. Strong, like their father, but with a will of their own."

Bastian's eyes met mine, something unreadable flickering in their depths. "I'll do whatever it takes to protect them, Adelaide. To protect you. I hope you believe that."

I wanted to say that I did, but the words wouldn't come. Instead, I nodded, my heart a whirlwind of emotions I couldn't begin to untangle.

As Bastian rose to fetch a blanket from the carriage, the wind picked up, bringing with it a sudden chill. I wrapped my arms around myself, watching him walk away, my mind a whirl of conflicting emotions. But just as I was beginning to make sense of it all, a sharp, violent cramp seized my abdomen.

The pain was unlike anything I had ever felt before—a stabbing, twisting agony that left me breathless. I gasped, clutching my stomach as the world tilted around me. The cramp hit again, harder this time, and I doubled over, my vision blurring with tears.

"Bastian!" I cried out, my voice strangled with pain.

He was at my side in an instant, his face pale with alarm as he knelt beside me. "Adelaide? What's wrong? What's happening?"

"I—I don't know," I managed to choke out, the pain so intense that I could hardly think. "It hurts... it hurts so much..."

Without another word, Bastian scooped me up in his arms, his expression one of grim determination. He carried me to the carriage, barking orders to the driver to take us back to his residence as quickly as possible. The urgency in his voice, the fear in his eyes, was almost enough to drown out the pain. Almost.

As the carriage sped through the streets, Bastian held me close, his hand gripping mine tightly. "It's going to be okay, Adelaide," he murmured, though his voice was thick with worry. "We're almost there. Just hold on."

His words were meant to comfort me, but all I could think about was the searing pain that refused to relent, the fear that something was terribly wrong. I had never seen Bastian like this—so vulnerable, so desperate—and it scared me almost as much as the pain itself.

When we finally arrived at his residence, Bastian didn't hesitate. He carried me straight inside, shouting for the doctor to be summoned. The staff scrambled to obey, their faces tight with worry as they hurried about. I could see the strain on Bastian's face, the way his jaw was clenched, his eyes dark with fear. This was no longer the confident, calculating duke I had come to know. This was a man terrified of losing something—or someone—he had only just begun to realize he cared about.

The doctor arrived quickly, his expression grave as he examined me. I clung to Bastian's hand, my nails digging into his skin as another wave of pain washed over me. I could hardly focus on what the doctor was saying, my mind clouded with fear and agony.

But one thing was clear: whatever was happening to me, it wasn't normal. And it was threatening to tear apart everything—everything I had been so desperate to keep at bay.

"Adelaide, stay with me," Bastian whispered, his voice breaking as he leaned down to press a kiss to my forehead. "Please, stay with me. We'll get through this. I promise."

I wanted to believe him, to find comfort in his words, but the pain was too much. All I could do was hold on, praying that this wasn't the end—that somehow, we would make it through this, together.

24

The Blood and Revelation

The room was suffused with a tense silence, broken only by the rustling of the doctor's tools as he worked quickly, his movements efficient and practiced. Bastian hovered nearby, his expression a mixture of worry and something deeper—something almost akin to fear. He held my hand tightly, as if letting go would somehow make everything unravel.

The doctor's brow furrowed as he inspected me, his hands gentle but firm as he pressed against my abdomen, his face betraying nothing. I winced as another sharp pain shot through me, biting down on my lip to stifle a cry. Bastian's grip on my hand tightened, and I could feel the tension radiating off him in waves.

"Your Grace," the doctor finally said, his voice grave, "I must ask you to step back."

Bastian hesitated, his eyes flicking to mine before he reluctantly released my hand and stepped aside. The doctor continued his examination, his expression growing more serious by the moment. Then, with a sharp intake of breath, he gently lifted the hem of my dress, revealing the crimson stain that had spread across the fabric.

A gasp escaped my lips, and Bastian's face drained of color. He took a step forward, his eyes wide with shock. "Is it... is she...?"

The doctor glanced up at him, his expression unreadable. "It appears the lady is bleeding, Your Grace. I must examine further to determine the cause."

My heart pounded in my chest, fear clawing at me as the doctor continued his work. I couldn't see Bastian's face, but I could feel the weight of his gaze on me, the tension in the room thickening with each passing second.

The minutes seemed to stretch into eternity as the doctor worked, his face a mask of concentration. Finally, he looked up, his expression softening slightly.

"Miss Blair," he began, his tone cautious, "I have determined that the bleeding is not from a miscarriage, as you may have feared. In fact, it appears that you have begun your monthly courses."

I blinked, the words not quite registering at first. "My... courses?"

"Yes," the doctor confirmed, his voice steady. "You are experiencing the onset of your monthly flow. It is a natural occurrence, and while the pain you are feeling is certainly distressing, it is not uncommon."

Relief flooded through me, a wave of emotion so overwhelming that I felt lightheaded. I wasn't pregnant. The realization hit me with the force of a crashing wave, and for a moment, I was lost in the tumult of feelings that followed. Relief, yes, but also something else—something I hadn't expected. A deep, aching sadness that settled in my chest, making it hard to breathe.

I wasn't pregnant. There was no child, no life growing within me. The very thing I had feared for so long, the thing I had tried to deny and resist, was now gone. And with it, a strange sense of loss that I couldn't quite explain.

But as I looked up at Bastian, the relief I felt was tempered by the sight of his face—pale, drawn, and filled with a deep, unspoken pain. His eyes were dark with disappointment, his expression one of profound hurt. He looked as though the ground had been ripped out from beneath him, as though the very foundation of his world had crumbled.

"There's no baby," I whispered, more to myself than to him.

Bastian's jaw tightened, his hands clenching into fists at his sides. "No," he said, his voice barely audible. "No, there isn't."

The doctor, sensing the tension between us, quietly excused himself, leaving the room with a promise to return later. The door clicked shut behind him, and the silence that followed was deafening.

I didn't know what to say, how to bridge the chasm that had opened between us. The man who had been so full of hope, who had spoken so tenderly to a child that didn't exist, was now standing before me, shattered and vulnerable in a way I had never seen before.

"Bastian..." I began, but the words caught in my throat. What could I say? What comfort could I offer to a man who had pinned his hopes on something that had never been real?

He turned away from me, his shoulders tense, his head bowed. "I thought..." He trailed off, his voice thick with emotion. "I thought there was a chance. That we... that you and I..."

His words broke off, and he let out a bitter laugh, shaking his head as if trying to rid himself of the thoughts that plagued him. "I must have been a fool."

"No," I said quickly, reaching out to him, but he flinched away, refusing to meet my gaze.

"I wanted to believe it," he continued, his voice low and pained. "I wanted to believe that there was something good—something pure—that could come out of all this. A child. Our child. But it was all just... a lie."

The anguish in his voice cut through me like a knife, and I felt my own tears welling up, stinging my eyes. "I never meant to lie to you, Bastian," I whispered. "I never wanted to hurt you."

He finally looked at me, his eyes filled with a deep, aching sorrow. "And yet, here we are."

The room seemed to close in around us, the air heavy with the weight of unspoken words, of dreams that had been dashed. I had been so focused on my own fears, my own need for control, that I had never stopped to consider what this might mean for him. For us.

The silence stretched on, filled with the ghosts of what might have been. Finally, Bastian spoke, his voice hollow. "You should rest, Adelaide. I'll have the carriage take you back to Windermere."

I wanted to protest, to say that I didn't want to leave things like this, but the look in his eyes told me that there was no point. He needed time, just as I did. Time to process what had happened, to come to terms with the reality we now faced.

He left the room without another word, and I was left alone, the echoes of our conversation ringing in my ears. I wasn't pregnant. The truth of it was both a blessing and a curse, a relief that was tainted by the knowledge of the pain it had caused.

As I lay back against the pillows, exhaustion washing over me, I couldn't help but wonder what the future would hold for us now. Bastian and I had been drawn together by a series of events neither of us could control, and now that the foundation of that bond had been stripped away, I was left with nothing but uncertainty.

But one thing was clear: the path ahead would not be easy. For either of us.

25

The Baby's Room

The days that followed were marked by a heavy, oppressive silence. Bastian had all but vanished from my life, retreating into the shadows of his estate, leaving me to wrestle with the conflicting emotions that churned within me. At first, I told myself that this was for the best—that his absence would allow me the space I needed to think, to heal. But as the hours turned into days, I couldn't shake the feeling that something important had been left unresolved.

I felt strange because there was no baby in my womb. It felt like something was missing. Maybe I was just like Bastian and started to think that there was Bastian's child in my belly and that I was really pregnant. Maybe I was imagining my belly growing so big in a few weeks that I couldn't hide it. But when I wasn't pregnant, I had to accept the fact that our baby didn't exist. Strangely enough, I felt disappointed.

Despite everything that had happened, I found myself missing his presence. His intensity, his determination—even his infuriating stubbornness. There was something about him that had woven itself into the fabric of my life, something I hadn't fully appreciated until now. And the thought of him suffering alone, nursing his disappointment and pain, gnawed at me in a way I hadn't anticipated.

I knew I needed to confront my feelings, to see him and speak the words that had been trapped in my chest since that day. And so, with a resolve that surprised even me, I decided to visit Bastian at his estate.

The carriage ride to Lightwood Manor was tense, the countryside passing by in a blur as I rehearsed what I would say. I imagined all the ways the conversation might go—how he might react, what I would do if he remained distant and cold. But nothing could prepare me for what I found when I arrived.

The manor loomed ahead, its imposing structure a stark contrast to the lush greenery that surrounded it. I stepped out of the carriage, my heart pounding with a mix of determination and trepidation. The butler, Alfred, met me at the door, his expression carefully neutral as he bowed and led me inside.

"Miss Blair," he greeted me with a respectful nod. "How may I assist you today?"

"I've come to see the Duke," I replied, my voice steadier than I felt. "I need to speak with him."

Alfred hesitated, a shadow passing over his face. "I'm afraid His Grace is not receiving visitors at the moment."

A pang of disappointment lanced through me, but I refused to be deterred. "Please, Alfred. I just need a moment with him. It's important."

The butler's eyes softened slightly, a flicker of sympathy in his gaze. "I understand, Miss Blair, but His Grace has been... unwell since the incident. He has requested to be left alone."

The words hit me harder than I expected, a knot of guilt tightening in my chest. "Unwell? Has he been ill?"

"Not in the physical sense, Miss," Alfred said quietly, his tone hesitant. "It is his spirit that is wounded. He has taken the news of your condition very hard."

I looked away, a fresh wave of guilt washing over me. "I never meant to hurt him," I whispered, more to myself than to Alfred.

"I know that, Miss Blair," Alfred replied gently. "But I believe His Grace needs time to come to terms with what has happened."

I nodded, swallowing against the lump in my throat. "But I must see him, Alfred. Please."

The butler seemed to consider my words for a long moment before he sighed, his shoulders sagging slightly. "Very well, Miss Blair. If you'll follow me."

He led me through the quiet halls of the manor, the grand rooms echoing with a silence that felt almost unnatural. I had visited Lightwood Manor before, but it had never felt this cold, this empty. Alfred guided me to a part of the house I had never seen, down a corridor that seemed removed from the rest of the manor's grandeur.

We stopped before a door at the end of the hall, and Alfred hesitated before turning to me. "This is where His Grace prepared a room for the child," he said softly. "He spent many evenings here, planning and preparing for the arrival of the little one."

I stared at the door, a sense of dread settling over me. "A room... for the child?"

Alfred nodded, his expression somber. "Yes, Miss Blair. He wanted everything to be perfect."

With a trembling hand, I reached for the door and pushed it open. The sight that greeted me was a punch to the gut, knocking the breath from my lungs. The room was small but beautifully appointed, every detail meticulously chosen. A cradle made of polished wood stood in the corner, draped with soft linens. A rocking chair sat beside it, a hand-knit blanket draped over the back. Toys were arranged neatly on a shelf, and the walls were painted a soft, calming blue.

I took a step inside, my hand flying to my mouth as I took it all in. Bastian had done this. He had created this room for a child that would never exist. The realization hit me with the force of a tidal wave, drowning me in a mixture of sorrow and regret.

"He was so certain," Alfred murmured from the doorway. "So certain that the child would come. I've never seen him so... hopeful."

I turned to look at the butler, my eyes filling with tears. "Why didn't he tell me?"

"I believe he wanted it to be a surprise," Alfred said gently. "A way to show you that he was committed, that he was ready to be a father."

My chest tightened, and I felt a sob rising in my throat. "I didn't know," I whispered, my voice breaking. "I didn't realize how much it meant to him."

Alfred stepped forward, his expression kind but firm. "Miss Blair, His Grace has been many things in his life—cold, calculating, distant. But this was the first time I've seen him truly want something for someone else. It wasn't just about the child. It was about you."

The tears spilled over, and I sank into the rocking chair, my hands trembling as I clutched the blanket. "I never meant for this to happen," I choked out. "I never meant to hurt him."

"I know," Alfred said softly. "But perhaps it isn't too late."

I looked up at him, my vision blurred by tears. "What do you mean?"

"He may be hurt, but he's not beyond reach," Alfred replied. "If you speak to him—if you truly open your heart to him—there's still a chance. A chance for something real."

I sat there, the weight of Alfred's words settling over me like a heavy cloak. Could it be possible? Could there still be a chance for Bastian and me to find something real, something lasting, despite all that had happened?

"I'll try," I whispered, my voice barely audible.

Alfred gave me a small, encouraging smile. "That's all he needs, Miss Blair. A chance."

With that, the butler turned and quietly left the room, leaving me alone in the space that Bastian had so lovingly prepared. I looked around, my heart aching with a sorrow I hadn't fully realized I was capable of feeling. This room was a testament to the man I had only just begun to understand—the man who had hidden his hope, his desire for something more, beneath a veneer of control and power.

I rose from the chair and walked to the cradle, running my fingers over the smooth wood. I could picture him here, standing where I stood now, imagining a future that would never be. The thought brought fresh tears to my eyes, but along with the sorrow, there was something else—a flicker of hope.

I couldn't change the past, couldn't undo the hurt we had caused each other. But maybe, just maybe, there was still a way forward. A way to take the pieces of what had been broken and build something new.

I wiped my tears and took a deep breath, the resolve I had felt earlier returning with renewed strength. I would find Bastian. I would make him listen, make him see that despite everything, we still had a chance. It was time to stop running, to stop hiding from the feelings I had kept buried for so long.

26

A Confidante's Counsel

The weight of what I had seen in the nursery at Lightwood Manor lingered with me as I returned home. The carefully chosen toys, the rocking chair, the crib—it was all a testament to the hope Bastian had held, a hope I had never realized existed. My heart ached with the knowledge that I had hurt him in ways I hadn't fully understood.

But more than that, I was beginning to realize just how much Bastian had come to mean to me. The man who had initially frightened me with his coldness and manipulation had shown a different side—a side that cared deeply, that wanted a future with me, and possibly with our child. The conflict within me was overwhelming, and I knew I couldn't sort through it alone.

There was only one person I could turn to for guidance: Anne, my elder sister. Anne had always been the level-headed one, the one I could confide in when my emotions became too tangled to untwist on my own.

I found her in the garden, enjoying a rare moment of solitude as she tended to the roses. Her auburn hair glinted in the sunlight, and there was a serene expression on her face as she gently pruned the flowers. For a moment, I hesitated, unsure of how to begin. But Anne must have sensed my presence, for she turned to me with a smile that quickly faded as she saw the turmoil in my eyes.

"Adelaide," she said softly, setting down her shears. "What's wrong?"

I bit my lip, the words caught in my throat. But Anne had always been perceptive, and she reached out to take my hand, leading me to a nearby bench where we could sit together.

"It's Bastian," I finally managed to say, my voice trembling. "I... I don't know what to do, Anne. I'm so confused."

Anne's expression softened with understanding. "Tell me what's troubling you, dearest. I'm here to listen."

I took a deep breath, trying to steady my nerves. "I need to tell you everything, Anne. The whole truth—things I've been too afraid to admit, even to myself."

Her eyes widened slightly, but she nodded, her hand squeezing mine in silent encouragement.

"It started that night at the kingdom's anniversary ball," I began, my voice barely above a whisper. "I drank too much after seeing Colin with another woman... and somehow, I ended up in Duke Bastian's bed."

Anne's breath hitched, her grip tightening on my hand. "Adelaide..."

"I didn't remember anything," I rushed on, the words tumbling out as I tried to get it all out before I lost my nerve. "Not until I woke up the next morning and found myself naked in his bed, with no idea how I got there. I panicked, and I ran. I wanted to forget it ever happened."

Anne stared at me, her eyes wide with shock. "And Bastian... he found you?"

"Yes," I admitted, tears stinging my eyes. "He sent a marriage proposal to our home, convinced that I was carrying his child. He thought that... that something happened that night, and he wanted to protect me and our supposed baby."

Anne's hand flew to her mouth, her face pale with disbelief. "Adelaide... you've been carrying this secret alone all this time? Why didn't you tell me?"

"I was terrified, Anne," I confessed, my voice breaking. "I didn't know what to do. And then, when I realized I wasn't pregnant, I thought it would all go away, that he'd leave me alone. But instead, Bastian suddenly disappeared."

"Disappeared?" Anne echoed, her voice filled with concern. "What do you mean?"

I swallowed hard, trying to keep my emotions in check. "After he found out that I wasn't pregnant, he vanished from my life. No letters, no visits—

nothing. I thought he had finally given up on me, that he had moved on. But when I went to his manor, I found out that he had been preparing a nursery, planning for a child that wasn't even real."

"The nursery?" Anne echoed, her brow furrowing in confusion.

"He had a room prepared," I explained, my voice growing thick with emotion. "A room for the baby he was so certain we were going to have. He planned it all, Anne, right down to the smallest detail. He was so hopeful, so sure, and I... I didn't realize how much it meant to him."

Anne's eyes softened with sympathy as she squeezed my hand. "Oh, Adelaide..."

"I never thought he was capable of such tenderness," I continued, my thoughts spilling out in a rush. "I thought he was only interested in control, in having things his way. But now, I'm not so sure. I think... I think I might have misjudged him."

Anne was silent for a moment, her expression a mixture of shock, sorrow, and something else—something deeper. "Adelaide, I had no idea you were going through all of this alone. You should have come to me."

"I know," I whispered, guilt washing over me. "But I didn't want to drag you into my mess. I didn't want you to think less of me."

Anne's eyes softened, and she pulled me into a tight embrace. "You're my sister, Adelaide. I would never think less of you. I'm just so sorry you felt like you had to carry this burden alone."

I clung to her, the weight of my secrets finally lifting as I allowed myself to lean on her support. "I'm so confused, Anne. I don't know what to do. Part of me is still scared, still unsure if I can trust Bastian. But another part of me... it's beginning to care for him, more than I ever expected."

Anne pulled back slightly, her hands resting on my shoulders as she looked into my eyes. "Adelaide, it sounds like Bastian has shown you a part of himself that he doesn't reveal to many. And it also sounds like you've begun to see him in a new light."

"I don't know what to do," I repeated, my voice trembling. "I don't know if I can trust him, but I can't deny that he cares about me—about us."

Anne smiled softly, her eyes filled with a wisdom that only an elder sister could possess. "Adelaide, love isn't always simple or easy, especially when there's been so much pain and misunderstanding. But I think you need to ask yourself one important question: Do you believe that Bastian truly cares for you? Not just as a means to an end, but as a person?"

I hesitated, thinking back to the way Bastian had looked at me, the way he had spoken to the child he believed we were going to have. There had been genuine emotion in his eyes, a vulnerability that I had never seen before.

"Yes," I admitted quietly. "I do think he cares. I think he's been trying to show me that in his own way, but I've been too afraid to see it."

Anne's smile grew, and she reached out to tuck a loose strand of hair behind my ear. "Then maybe it's time to stop letting fear hold you back, Adelaide. You're stronger than you know, and if your heart is telling you that Bastian is worth the risk, then perhaps it's time to trust that."

Her words resonated deep within me, and I felt a sense of clarity begin to emerge from the fog of confusion. She was right—I had been letting fear dictate my actions, afraid to open myself up to the possibility of love because of the pain it might bring. But Bastian had shown me a different side of himself, a side that was capable of love, of tenderness, and I couldn't ignore that.

"Thank you, Anne," I whispered, my eyes filling with tears. "I don't know what I'd do without you."

Anne pulled me into a comforting embrace, her warmth enveloping me like a protective shield. "You'll always have me, dearest. But remember, the decision is yours to make. Follow your heart, and everything else will fall into place."

I nodded, feeling a sense of resolve settle over me. I knew what I had to do. It was time to stop running, to stop letting fear keep me from the chance at happiness that was right in front of me.

But even as I made up my mind, a new worry crept in. The rumors that had begun circulating among society were growing louder, more insistent. Whispers about that night with Bastian, about the scandal that would surely follow if the truth were to come out. I had tried to ignore them, to push them aside as idle gossip, but I couldn't deny that the rumors were starting to take on a life of their own.

27

The Whispering Winds

The winds of gossip began to swirl almost immediately after my conversation with Anne. What had started as faint whispers in the drawing rooms of the ton soon became a roaring storm, threatening to tear apart everything I had fought so hard to protect. My night with Duke Bastian had become the talk of society, with each retelling more embellished and malicious than the last.

It started with sidelong glances at social gatherings, quiet murmurs behind gloved hands, and subtle but cutting comments about the "unexpected" nature of my engagement to the Duke of Lightwood. But as the rumors grew, so did the cruelty of the tales being spun.

It wasn't long before the rumors took on a life of their own. Some claimed that I had shamelessly pursued Bastian, luring him into a scandalous affair to secure his proposal. Others whispered that I had seduced him, trapping him in a web of deceit with the promise of a child that never existed. The most vicious of all implied that I had been involved with multiple men that night and had simply chosen Bastian as the most advantageous target.

Each day brought a fresh wave of speculation, and I could feel the walls closing in around me as the scandal intensified. My every move was scrutinized, every gesture analyzed for signs of guilt. It was as though society had decided my fate long before I had a chance to defend myself.

Even the invitations that had once flooded in began to dwindle, replaced by cold shoulders and icy receptions. Those who had once welcomed me into their homes now kept their distance, afraid that the taint of scandal would spread to them by association. The isolation was suffocating, and I felt more alone than ever before.

One afternoon, as I walked through the market square, I could feel the weight of the stares pressing down on me. The usual buzz of activity seemed to falter as I passed, and I caught snatches of conversations that made my heart ache.

"Such a shame... she seemed like such a sweet girl..."

"They say the Duke only proposed because he had no choice. Imagine the disgrace..."

"Her poor family... what will become of them if this continues?"

The words cut deep, each one a reminder of how quickly society could turn on someone they had once embraced. I kept my head held high, refusing to let them see how much their whispers affected me, but inside, I was crumbling.

As I hurried past a group of women who were openly gossiping about me, I caught sight of Lady Abigail, one of the most influential women in society. She had always been a pillar of propriety, someone whose approval could make or break a young lady's prospects. But now, as she met my gaze, there was no warmth in her eyes—only cold judgment.

"Miss Blair," she said coolly, her voice loud enough to carry to those around her. "I trust you are... well?"

I forced a polite smile, even as my heart pounded in my chest. "Thank you for your concern, Lady Abigail. I am managing as best I can."

Her lips curved into a smile that didn't reach her eyes. "Indeed. I do hope the rumors circulating about you are... exaggerated. It would be such a pity for someone of your standing to fall from grace so spectacularly."

The thinly veiled threat in her words sent a shiver down my spine, but I refused to let her see my fear. "I assure you, Lady Abigail, I have always conducted myself with the utmost propriety."

"Of course," she replied, her tone dripping with insincerity. "But you know how these things can spiral out of control. A lady must be ever vigilant in guarding her reputation, lest it be tarnished beyond repair."

With that, she turned away, leaving me standing in the square with a sick feeling in the pit of my stomach. It was clear that the tide was turning against me, and I was running out of time to salvage my reputation.

As I made my way back home, the weight of the scandal pressed down on me like a suffocating blanket. I knew that I couldn't face this alone—not anymore. The rumors were too powerful, the judgment too swift. If I didn't find a way to turn the tide, everything I had worked for—everything my family had worked for—would be lost.

When I reached Windermere Manor, I found Anne waiting for me in the drawing room, her expression filled with concern. She had heard the rumors too, and I could see the worry etched in her features.

"Adelaide," she said softly, rising to meet me. "I've heard... things. The rumors, they're getting worse."

I nodded, the exhaustion evident in my voice. "I know, Anne. I can feel it—the way everyone looks at me, the way they talk about me. It's as if they've already decided that I'm guilty."

Anne's eyes filled with sympathy, and she took my hands in hers. "You don't have to go through this alone, Adelaide. We'll find a way to clear your name, to stop these rumors before they destroy everything."

"But how?" I asked, my voice trembling. "How do we fight something like this? It feels like the more I try to defend myself, the worse it gets."

Anne was silent for a moment, her gaze steady as she searched my face. "What about Bastian? Has he said anything? Surely he can help put an end to this."

I shook my head, frustration and fear mingling in my chest. "He's been... distant. After he found out I wasn't pregnant, he disappeared. I thought he had given up on me, but then I saw the nursery he had prepared. It's like he doesn't know what to do anymore, and neither do I."

Anne's brow furrowed in thought. "We need to talk to him, Adelaide. He's part of this too, and if anyone can help quash these rumors, it's him."

I knew she was right, but the thought of confronting Bastian, of asking for his help, filled me with dread. The last time we had spoken, I had seen a side of him that was vulnerable, uncertain—a side that had made me question everything I thought I knew about him. But now, with the walls closing in around me, I had no other choice.

"I'll speak to him," I said finally, my voice firm despite the fear gnawing at me. "I'll go to Lightwood Manor and ask him to help put an end to this."

Anne squeezed my hands, her gaze filled with determination. "We'll get through this, Adelaide. You're stronger than you think, and you're not alone in this fight."

I nodded, taking comfort in her words. But as I prepared to face the Duke of Lightwood once more, I couldn't shake the feeling that the winds of gossip had already set events in motion that I might not be able to stop.

The time for hiding was over. It was time to face the storm head-on, to confront the man who had unwittingly started it all, and to find a way to reclaim the life that was slipping through my fingers.

28

Facing the Storm

The decision to confront the rumors head-on was not one I made lightly. Every fiber of my being wanted to retreat, to hide away from the prying eyes and vicious tongues of high society. But as Anne had reminded me, courage was not the absence of fear, but the will to act despite it. With her unwavering support, I resolved to face the storm that threatened to engulf me.

The annual Solstice Gala was the most prestigious event of the season, attended by the crème de la crème of society. It was a night of opulence, of glittering gowns and sparkling jewels, of music and dance that lasted until the early hours of the morning. It was also the perfect stage upon which to make my stand.

As I prepared for the evening, I chose a gown that exuded elegance and strength—a deep sapphire silk that flowed like water with every step. The neckline was modest yet flattering, and the intricate silver embroidery caught the light with each movement. Anne helped arrange my hair into an intricate chignon, adorned with delicate pearl pins that had once belonged to our mother.

"You look stunning," Anne whispered, a proud smile gracing her lips as she adjusted a stray curl. "No one will be able to take their eyes off you."

I met her gaze in the mirror, drawing strength from her confidence. "Thank you, Anne. I couldn't do this without you."

She squeezed my shoulder gently. "You've always had this strength within you, Adelaide. Tonight, the world will see it too."

With a final deep breath, I descended the grand staircase of Windermere Manor, ready to face whatever awaited me.

The carriage ride to the Grand Hall was a blur of flickering streetlamps and the rhythmic clatter of hooves against cobblestone. As we approached the towering edifice, the sounds of laughter and music drifted through the night air, mingling with the soft glow of lanterns that lined the entrance.

Stepping out of the carriage, I felt the weight of countless eyes upon me. Whispers rippled through the crowd as I made my way up the marble steps, Anne by my side. But instead of shrinking beneath their scrutiny, I lifted my chin, meeting their gazes with unwavering resolve.

Inside, the ballroom was a symphony of color and light. Crystal chandeliers cast a warm glow over the sea of elegantly dressed guests, their laughter and conversation weaving a tapestry of sound that filled the expansive space. The orchestra played a lively waltz, and couples twirled gracefully across the polished floor.

As we entered, the chatter seemed to hush momentarily, all eyes turning towards us. I could feel the intensity of their stares, the unspoken questions and judgments that hung heavy in the air. But I refused to be intimidated. Instead, I allowed a serene smile to grace my lips, acknowledging the onlookers with a nod before making my way further into the room.

Lady Abigail, ever the sentinel of propriety, approached with a calculated smile. "Miss Blair, how lovely to see you this evening. Your gown is exquisite."

"Thank you, Lady Abigail," I replied, matching her composed demeanor. "The event is truly splendid. The decorations are particularly breathtaking this year."

She raised an eyebrow, perhaps taken aback by my forthrightness. "Indeed. It's always a highlight of the season."

There was a brief pause, the unspoken tension palpable. I could sense her probing, waiting for a misstep, an admission of guilt. But I held my ground, refusing to give her the satisfaction.

"Have you had the chance to enjoy the gardens?" I inquired, steering the conversation away from treacherous waters. "I've heard the blooms are exceptional this time of year."

Lady Abigail's smile turned sharper, her eyes narrowing slightly. "Not as exceptional as the latest gossip, I'm afraid."

My heart skipped a beat, but I kept my expression neutral. "Gossip tends to be exaggerated, Lady Abigail. I've learned to pay it little mind."

"Oh, have you?" she replied, her voice dripping with condescension. "It's a shame others don't share your philosophy. The rumors about you and Duke Lightwood have certainly taken on a life of their own."

I remained silent, my pulse quickening as she continued.

"Speaking of the Duke," she said with a pointed look, "it seems he's chosen to distance himself from this scandal. Perhaps he's already moved on."

I forced myself to remain calm, despite the knot tightening in my chest. "I wouldn't presume to know the Duke's thoughts or actions, Lady Abigail."

She leaned in slightly, her voice dropping to a conspiratorial whisper. "Well, it's not just rumors anymore, Miss Blair. I've heard from reliable sources that Duke Bastian is to be married soon... to Lady Isabella."

The air seemed to leave the room in that moment, my breath catching in my throat. Lady Isabella—one of the most prominent members of the royal family, and a woman long rumored to be Bastian's intended. The news hit me like a physical blow, but I couldn't let it show.

"Is that so?" I asked, my voice steady despite the turmoil within.

"Yes," Lady Abigail said with a smirk. "It appears that the scandal involving you and the Duke has forced the royal family's hand. They couldn't allow such a match to be tainted, so they've hastened the arrangement with Lady Isabella. Some say that you spread the rumors yourself, hoping to trap the Duke into marriage."

The accusation was like a slap to the face, but I refused to give her the satisfaction of seeing my hurt. Instead, I met her gaze with a calmness I didn't feel. "That is a baseless and cruel accusation, Lady Abigail. I would never resort to such underhanded tactics."

She tilted her head, as if considering my words. "Perhaps. But perception is reality in our world, Miss Blair. And the reality is that the Duke is soon to be married to someone far more suitable than you."

The words stung, but I held my ground. "I suppose time will reveal the truth, won't it?"

Lady Abigail seemed disappointed by my lack of reaction, but she didn't press further. With a curt nod, she turned and swept away, leaving me standing alone with the weight of her words pressing down on me.

As I stood there, I realized just how dire my situation had become. Bastian's disappearance from the public eye, combined with the rumors of his impending marriage to Lady Isabella, had placed me in an impossible position. The scandal had taken on a life of its own, and now I was being accused of trying to snatch the Duke from his rightful bride.

But I would not be cowed. I would not allow the whispers and stares to dictate my life. As much as Lady Abigail's words had shaken me, I knew I had to remain strong.

Gathering my resolve, I moved through the ballroom with my head held high, refusing to let the scandalous whispers define me. Every gaze that met mine, every whispered word that followed in my wake, only fueled my determination.

I sought out Anne, who had been watching from a distance, concern etched on her face. As I approached, she took my hands in hers, squeezing them gently.

"I heard what she said," Anne whispered, her eyes searching mine. "Are you alright?"

I forced a small smile, though my heart still ached. "I'm fine. Lady Abigail was just doing what she does best—stirring the pot."

Anne's gaze softened with sympathy. "This is all so unfair, Adelaide. You don't deserve any of this."

"Perhaps not," I replied, my voice firm. "But I won't let them see me falter. I won't give them the satisfaction."

Anne nodded, pride flickering in her eyes. "You're stronger than they'll ever know."

The evening continued, and though the weight of Lady Abigail's words lingered, I refused to let them break me. I danced, I conversed, I smiled—all while the storm of rumors swirled around me. I would not be swept away by it.

29

An Unexpected Ally

The days following the Solstice Gala were a blur of tense moments and whispered rumors, each one more vicious than the last. Lady Abigail's words haunted me, lingering in my mind like a dark cloud I couldn't shake. The thought of Bastian marrying Lady Isabella, combined with the accusation that I had somehow orchestrated the scandal to trap him, left me feeling cornered and isolated.

But just when I thought the walls were closing in on me, an unexpected ally stepped forward.

It happened on a dreary afternoon, when the sky was heavy with the threat of rain. I had just returned from a walk in the garden, seeking a moment of peace amidst the growing turmoil. As I entered the drawing room, I was surprised to find Colin waiting for me, his expression a mix of concern and determination.

"Adelaide," he greeted me, his voice low and serious. "We need to talk."

"Colin?" I said, taken aback by his sudden appearance. "What are you doing here?"

He didn't answer right away, instead gesturing for me to sit down. His eyes were filled with a quiet intensity I hadn't seen in him before, and it made my heart skip a beat.

"I've heard the rumors," Colin finally said, his voice laced with anger. "About you and Bastian. About the so-called scandal."

I sighed, sinking into the chair opposite him. "Everyone has heard them, Colin. They're spreading like wildfire, and there's nothing I can do to stop it."

Colin's jaw tightened, and he leaned forward, his hands clasped together as if trying to rein in his frustration. "This isn't right, Adelaide. You don't deserve this. I can't stand by and watch while your reputation is torn apart."

His words caught me off guard, and I looked at him, truly looked at him, for the first time in what felt like ages. There was a fierce protectiveness in his eyes, a loyalty that warmed something deep within me. For so long, I had thought of Colin as my dearest friend, someone I could always rely on, but I had never expected him to step into the fray like this.

"What are you saying?" I asked quietly, unsure of where this conversation was headed.

"I'm saying that I want to help," Colin replied, his voice firm. "I've already spoken to a few key people in society—those who hold sway over public opinion. I've told them that the rumors are baseless, that you would never do what they're accusing you of."

I blinked in surprise, my heart swelling with gratitude. "You did that? But Colin, what about your own reputation? People might start talking about you too, accusing you of being involved in this mess."

He waved off my concern. "I don't care what they say about me. What matters is that you don't face this alone."

His words touched me more deeply than I could express, and for a moment, I felt a flicker of the old feelings I had once harbored for him. Colin had always been there for me, always by my side through thick and thin. And now, when the world seemed determined to tear me down, he was standing up for me in a way I hadn't anticipated.

"Colin," I whispered, my voice trembling with emotion. "I don't know what to say. Thank you."

He smiled, a gentle, reassuring smile that made my heart ache with nostalgia. "You don't have to say anything, Adelaide. I just want you to know that I'm here for you, no matter what."

There was a pause, a moment of silence that seemed to stretch on forever.

I could feel the weight of unspoken words between us, the remnants of a connection that had never fully faded. For a fleeting moment, I wondered if things could have been different, if I had chosen a different path, a different person to place my hopes in.

But then reality came crashing back, the memory of Bastian's disappearance and the scandal that had ensued. My heart was a tangled mess of emotions, torn between the safety and comfort of Colin's loyalty and the unresolved feelings I still harbored for the man who had left me to face this storm alone.

"I don't want you to get hurt," I said softly, my voice barely above a whisper. "You've always been so good to me, Colin. I couldn't bear it if you got dragged into this mess because of me."

He reached out, taking my hand in his, and the warmth of his touch sent a shiver through me. "Adelaide, I'm not doing this out of obligation. I'm doing it because I care about you. Because I... well, because I never stopped caring."

His confession left me breathless, my heart pounding in my chest. I had always known that Colin had feelings for me, feelings that went beyond friendship, but hearing him say it so plainly now, in the midst of everything that was happening, stirred something deep within me.

"I care about you too, Colin," I admitted, my voice trembling. "But things are so complicated right now. I don't know what to do, or what I even want."

He nodded, understanding in his eyes. "I'm not asking for anything, Adelaide. I just want you to know that you're not alone. Whatever happens, I'll be here, and I'll do everything I can to protect you."

Tears welled up in my eyes, and I squeezed his hand, grateful beyond words for his support. But even as I leaned on Colin's strength, I couldn't shake the conflict that churned within me. The loyalty and affection I felt for him were real, but they were tangled up in the unresolved feelings I still had for Bastian.

As much as Colin's presence comforted me, it also reminded me of the choices I had made, the paths I had taken that had led me to this point. I cared for Colin deeply, but was it enough? Or was my heart still too entangled with thoughts of Bastian to see clearly?

The days that followed were filled with Colin's quiet, steadfast support. He attended social events with me, shielding me from the worst of the rumors, offering a steady arm to lean on when the weight of it all became too much. But his presence also complicated matters, reigniting feelings I thought I had long buried.

I was touched by his loyalty, by the way he stood by me when so many others had turned away. But the more time I spent with Colin, the more conflicted I became. Was I clinging to him out of gratitude and a longing for stability? Or was there something more, something deeper that I had been too blind to see?

And then, of course, there was the specter of Bastian, always lingering at the edges of my thoughts. His absence loomed large, a constant reminder of the unresolved emotions that still held me in their grip. I couldn't help but wonder where he was, what he was thinking, and whether he would ever return to face the consequences of the scandal we had inadvertently created.

As the days turned into weeks, I knew I couldn't continue like this. I had to make a choice, to confront my feelings head-on and decide what it was that I truly wanted. Colin had been an unexpected ally, a beacon of support in a time of turmoil, but the decision was mine to make.

Would I choose the safety and loyalty of the man who had always been there for me? Or would I wait for the return of the one who had left me in the storm, but who still held a piece of my heart?

The storm may have raged on, but the real battle was the one within myself. And until I faced it, I would never find the peace I so desperately sought.

30

The Storm of Accusations

The rumors were like wildfire, spreading faster than I could have ever imagined. Colin's attempts to shield me from the worst of it had only fueled the gossip, turning the whispers into something far more vicious. Now, they said I was playing a dangerous game, toying with men's affections—first with Bastian, and now with Colin. The idea that I was some sort of scheming temptress made my skin crawl, but it was the world I found myself trapped in.

I retreated into the safety of Windermere Manor, refusing to go out. I couldn't bear the thought of facing the judgmental stares, the mocking smiles, and the cutting remarks. My parents were mortified, their embarrassment a palpable weight that hung over the household. The once warm and bustling manor now felt cold, like a fortress of shame.

It was Anne who finally broke through the fog of my despair. She found me in the sitting room, staring blankly out the window, my mind numb from the relentless onslaught of rumors.

"Adelaide," she said gently, sitting beside me and taking my hand. "You can't go on like this. It's not good for you, and it's not going to make the rumors stop."

I shook my head, my voice barely above a whisper. "What else can I do, Anne? They've already decided who I am, what I am. Nothing I say or do will change that."

Anne squeezed my hand, her gaze filled with sympathy and determination. "You need to talk to Bastian. He's at the center of this as much as you are. You can't let the rumors fester without confronting him."

The thought of facing Bastian again filled me with dread, but Anne's words were logical. I couldn't let this situation continue to spiral out of control without at least trying to find some resolution. If anyone had the power to stop the rumors, it was Bastian.

With Anne's encouragement, I gathered what remained of my courage and made the decision to visit Bastian's residence. The carriage ride to Lightwood Manor felt interminable, the clatter of hooves on cobblestone doing little to calm my racing thoughts. I tried to prepare myself for what I might say, but the words kept slipping away, leaving me with nothing but a heavy sense of unease.

When the carriage finally pulled up to the grand entrance of Lightwood Manor, my heart pounded in my chest. I stepped out, drawing in a deep breath as I approached the door. Alfred, Bastian's ever-loyal butler, greeted me with a polite nod and led me inside.

But nothing could have prepared me for what I found.

There, standing in the grand foyer, was Bastian—his hand resting lightly on the arm of Lady Isabella. She was every bit as regal and poised as the rumors had made her out to be, her beauty undeniable, her presence commanding. Seeing them together, so close, so comfortable, made something inside me twist painfully.

"Adelaide," Bastian greeted me, his tone measured, his eyes unreadable. "I wasn't expecting you."

I forced myself to remain composed, even as the sight of them together sent my emotions into turmoil. "I'm sure you weren't," I replied coolly, my gaze flicking to Lady Isabella before returning to Bastian. "But we need to talk."

Lady Isabella, sensing the tension, gracefully excused herself, leaving Bastian and me alone. He motioned for me to follow him into a more private room, but I couldn't bear the thought of sitting down, of pretending this was some civil conversation.

"No," I said, my voice hardening as I stood my ground in the foyer. "We can talk here."

Bastian paused, a flicker of something—confusion, perhaps—crossing his features. "Very well. What is it that you need to discuss?"

I took a deep breath, my heart pounding with anger and hurt. "I know what you've been doing, Your Grace. Don't think for a moment that I'm naive enough to believe otherwise."

He frowned, clearly taken aback by my sudden accusation. "What are you talking about, Adelaide?"

I clenched my fists, the words spilling out before I could stop them. "You've been spreading those rumors, haven't you? You wanted to ruin my good name, to clear the path for your marriage to Lady Isabella. All of this—everything that's happened—it's because I wasn't pregnant, isn't it?"

His eyes widened, shock and anger flashing across his face. "That's not true. I would never—"

"Don't lie to me!" I interrupted, my voice rising as the pain and frustration I had kept bottled up finally burst free. "You've made me a laughingstock, a scandal. All because I didn't give you the child you wanted. Now you're clearing your name so you can marry Lady Isabella without any baggage."

"Adelaide, stop," Bastian said, his voice firm, but I refused to listen.

"No, you stop!" I shot back, my voice trembling with emotion. "You've taken everything from me—my reputation, my peace, my sense of self. And now you stand here, with her, as if none of it matters."

Bastian's expression softened, a look of genuine hurt crossing his features. "Adelaide, I haven't spread any rumors. I haven't done anything to harm you. I wanted to protect you, to keep you safe—"

"Protect me?" I repeated, my voice dripping with bitterness. "By disappearing? By leaving me to face this alone while you entertain the idea of marrying another?"

He reached out as if to comfort me, but I took a step back, shaking my head. "Don't, Bastian. I don't need your explanations. I just needed to hear it from your own lips that I meant nothing to you."

"You mean everything to me," he insisted, his voice strained with emotion.

"Please, just let me explain—"

"I'm done listening to your explanations," I said, cutting him off as tears threatened to spill. "I'm done with all of this."

Without another word, I turned on my heel and fled from Lightwood Manor, my chest tight with a mix of anger and heartbreak. I barely noticed Alfred as he hurried to open the door for me, nor did I acknowledge the concerned looks from the staff as I made my way back to the waiting carriage.

As soon as the door closed behind me, I broke down, the tears I had fought so hard to hold back finally spilling over. The carriage jolted forward, and I clutched at the seat, my body shaking with sobs. I had been foolish to think that Bastian could ever care for me, foolish to believe that there could be anything more between us than a mistake and a scandal.

The journey back to Windermere Manor felt endless, the weight of my emotions pressing down on me with every passing moment. I had gone to confront Bastian, hoping for answers, for some kind of resolution, but all I had found was more pain, more confusion.

By the time I reached home, I was drained, both physically and emotionally. I couldn't even bring myself to explain what had happened to Anne, who was waiting anxiously for my return. I simply nodded to her, my face streaked with tears, and retreated to my room, where I could cry in the privacy of my own misery.

The storm had taken everything from me, and now, even my heart lay shattered in its wake.

31

The Final Ultimatum

The morning after my heartbreaking encounter with Bastian, I awoke to a heavy silence that seemed to hang over Windermere Manor like a dark cloud. The usual bustle of servants and the warm chatter of family life were absent, replaced by a tension that made it difficult to breathe. I knew that the events of the previous day had deeply unsettled my family, and I braced myself for what was to come.

It wasn't long before my parents summoned me to the drawing room for a family discussion. As I entered, I found them already seated, their faces etched with worry. Anne stood by the window, her expression unreadable as she gazed out at the gardens beyond. My father, the Earl of Windermere, gestured for me to sit, his usually stern demeanor more intense than ever.

"Adelaide," my mother began, her voice trembling slightly as she folded her hands in her lap. "We've been talking, your father and I, and we believe it's time for you to consider a fresh start."

I sat down slowly, my heart sinking as I realized where this conversation was heading. "What do you mean, Mother?"

My father leaned forward, his gaze unwavering as he spoke. "The rumors have spiraled out of control, Adelaide. We've tried to protect you, but the truth is, you did spend that night with Duke Bastian. Society knows there's some truth to the rumors, and it's become impossible to stop the gossip."

I flinched at his words, the reminder of that night sending a fresh wave of shame through me. But before I could respond, my father continued, his voice firm and resolute.

"We've decided that it's best for you to leave London," he said. "To start anew, away from the prying eyes and cruel tongues of the ton."

"Leave London?" I repeated, disbelief flooding my voice. "Where would I go?"

"There's a village near the sea—Whitby," my father replied, his tone brooking no argument. "It's far enough from London that the rumors won't follow you. The people there are less concerned with high society's scandals. You could live a quiet life, far from all of this."

My heart pounded as I processed his words. Whitby was a small, picturesque village on the northern coast, known for its rugged beauty and simple way of life. It was the kind of place where one could disappear, where the past could be left behind. But the thought of leaving everything I knew, of abandoning my life in London, filled me with dread.

"There's also a man there," my father added, his voice growing even more insistent. "A respectable man, a widower who has been looking for a wife to help him raise his children. He's a good match, Adelaide. We've made inquiries, and we believe this is the best solution for you."

"A suitable match?" I echoed, my voice trembling. "You want me to marry a man I've never met, to hide away in some village because of a mistake I made?"

My father's expression softened slightly, but his resolve was clear. "I'm thinking of your future, Adelaide. The scandal here has made it nearly impossible for you to find a respectable match in London. Whitby offers you a chance to start over, to build a new life."

The words "start over" echoed in my mind, a mix of temptation and terror. I knew my father was trying to protect me, to shield me from the cruelty of society, but the idea of leaving everything behind—my family, my friends, and even Bastian—was unbearable.

"I can't," I whispered, shaking my head as tears welled up in my eyes. "I can't just leave, not like this. I know the rumors are terrible, and I know I've made mistakes, but running away won't solve anything. I need to clear my name, to face this head-on."

My father's eyes hardened, his voice taking on a tone of finality. "Adelaide, this is not just about you. This scandal affects all of us—our family's reputation, our standing in society. You need to understand that sometimes, starting over is the only way to move forward."

My mother reached out, placing a hand on my father's arm in a silent plea for gentleness. "Your father and I want what's best for you, darling. We're asking you to consider this for your own sake."

But I had already made up my mind. Despite everything that had happened, despite the heartbreak and the pain, I couldn't bring myself to leave. I couldn't admit it aloud, not even to myself, but the truth was I still loved Bastian. Even after all the accusations, even after seeing him with Lady Isabella, a part of me couldn't let go. And more than that, I wanted to prove to the world—and to myself—that I was more than the rumors that surrounded me.

"I'm staying," I said firmly, wiping away the tears that threatened to fall. "I'm staying in London, and I'm going to fight this. I can't run away from my problems, not this time."

My father's expression darkened, his disappointment clear. "You're making a mistake, Adelaide. This scandal won't just disappear because you wish it so. The damage has been done."

"I know," I replied, my voice resolute. "But it's my decision to make."

My father stood, his posture stiff with frustration. "Then you leave us no choice. If you insist on staying, you'll have to face the consequences on your own. We can't continue to shield you from the fallout."

His words cut deep, but I held my ground. "I understand, Father. But this is something I have to do."

My mother, her eyes filled with sorrow, looked at me with a mixture of love and helplessness. "We'll always support you, Adelaide, but if you ever change your mind... Whitby will be waiting."

I nodded, grateful for their understanding, even as I knew they were disappointed. The idea of leaving everything behind, of starting over in some remote village, was terrifying. But the thought of abandoning Bastian, of giving up on clearing my name, was even worse.

As the conversation ended and my parents left the room, I remained seated, alone with my thoughts. The path I had chosen was fraught with uncertainty and danger, but it was my path. I had made mistakes, and I would face the consequences, but I wouldn't run away. Not this time.

I was determined to fight for my name, my reputation, and my heart—even if it meant facing the storm alone.

32

A Desperate Decision

The days following my family's ultimatum were a blur of anxiety and dread. The rumors, which had already felt unbearable, somehow escalated even further, spiraling into wild and malicious stories that twisted the truth beyond recognition.

It seemed that everyone in London had something to say about Adelaide Blair. The whispers no longer stopped when I entered a room—instead, they seemed to grow louder, more vicious, as if the gossips fed off my presence. The once fleeting glances had turned into outright stares, and it felt as though the entire city was waiting with bated breath for my inevitable downfall.

One particularly cruel rumor reached me during a visit to a local shop, where I had hoped to escape the relentless scrutiny, if only for a moment. As I browsed the shelves, I overheard two women talking in hushed tones, their words cutting through the air like knives.

"They say she's desperate now," one of them whispered, her voice tinged with gleeful malice. "That she's been entertaining offers from every eligible man in London, hoping to secure a match before she's completely ruined."

Their words cut through me like a knife, leaving me reeling with a mixture of anger, hurt, and desperation. The rumors were spinning out of control, and the more I tried to stand firm, the more it seemed like the world was conspiring against me.

"But they say she's been begging every man in London to marry her," one

A DESPERATE DECISION

of them whispered, her voice full of glee. "Poor thing, she must be terrified of becoming a spinster with no prospects."

"And did you hear?" the other woman replied, her tone equally venomous. "The Duke Lightwood is to marry Lady Isabella. It's only a matter of time before the announcement is made. I heard that Miss Blair was trying to trap him, but it backfired. Poor Miss Blair—she's been cast aside like yesterday's news."

My heart sank as the words sank in. So the rumors about Bastian and Lady Isabella were true after all. The very thought made my chest tighten with a mix of anger, betrayal, and a deep, aching sadness.

I rushed out of the shop, the weight of the rumors pressing down on me like never before. As I returned to Windermere Manor, I felt more isolated and desperate than ever. The scandal had grown too large, too overwhelming for me to fight alone. And the more I tried to stand my ground, the more I realized just how little power I had against the tide of public opinion.

In the days that followed, the pressure only increased. My father's frustration with my refusal to leave for Whitby became more pronounced, and even Anne—my steadfast ally—began to worry that my determination to stay in London was leading me down a dangerous path. The whispers of my supposed desperation to find a husband had begun to surface among the few remaining suitors who dared to approach me, and I could see the pity in their eyes, the calculation as they weighed the benefits of tying themselves to a woman so embroiled in scandal.

It was during one of these suffocating days that a letter arrived at Windermere Manor. The envelope was plain, the handwriting unfamiliar, but the contents were clear: an offer of marriage from Mr. Timothy Crawford, a wealthy landowner with a solid, if unremarkable, reputation. He was not a man I had ever taken much notice of before, but now, his proposal was laid out before me, tempting in its promise of safety and stability.

When I returned to Windermere Manor, my parents were waiting for me in the drawing room, their expressions grave. The tension in the room was palpable, and I knew that whatever they had to say would be difficult to hear.

"Adelaide," my father began, his voice low and serious, "we've received a

145

letter. It's from Mr. Timothy Crawford, the widower from Whitby."

I blinked in surprise, remembering the name. Mr. Crawford was the man my parents had mentioned before, the one they believed would be a suitable match for me if I were to leave London and start anew in the countryside. He was a wealthy landowner, respected in his community, but most importantly, he was a man in need of a wife to help him raise his children.

"He's made a formal proposal," my mother added gently, as she handed me the letter. "He's offering you the chance to start fresh in Whitby, away from the scandal and the rumors."

I took the letter with trembling hands, scanning the neat, polite words. Mr. Crawford's offer was straightforward: he needed a wife, a mother for his five young sons, the youngest of whom was still a baby. In return, he offered me a life of stability, far from the prying eyes of London society.

"Five children?" I whispered, the enormity of the situation sinking in. "He wants me to help him raise five boys, one of them a baby?"

"Yes," my father confirmed, his tone firm. "He's a good man, Adelaide. He can offer you a respectable life in the countryside, away from all of this."

"But it's not the life I want," I protested, my voice cracking. "I don't know the first thing about raising children, let alone five. And to leave everything behind—my friends, my family—how can I do that?"

My father's expression hardened, his resolve clear. "This is your best option, Adelaide. The scandal here in London has made it nearly impossible for you to find a suitable match. Mr. Crawford's proposal is a chance for you to start over, to live a life free from the judgment of society."

"But at what cost?" I asked, feeling the weight of the decision pressing down on me. "Marrying a man I've never met, living in a place I've never been, taking on responsibilities I'm not prepared for—how can that be right?"

"The cost of peace," my father replied sternly. "The cost of a future that isn't overshadowed by the mistakes of the past."

My mother reached out, her hand warm on my arm. "Think about what this could mean, darling. You could leave all of this behind, live a quiet, dignified life in the countryside. You wouldn't have to face the whispers and stares anymore."

The idea was tempting, painfully so. The thought of escaping the relentless scrutiny, of finding refuge in the safety of a conventional marriage, was a balm to my frayed nerves. Mr. Crawford's proposal offered a way out, a way to put all of this behind me and begin anew.

But deep down, I knew that accepting his offer would mean sacrificing something far more important: my chance at true happiness. A marriage of convenience, no matter how respectable, would never fill the void that had been left by Bastian. It would never heal the wounds inflicted by the rumors, the scandal, and the heartbreak.

I could picture the life that awaited me in Whitby: days spent tending to five rambunctious boys, evenings by the fire in a small country home, far from the glittering lights of London. It was a life of stability, of respectability, but it was also a life of resignation, a life without the passion or love I had once dreamed of.

"I can't," I said finally, my voice trembling as I pushed the letter away. "I can't marry him."

My father's expression darkened, his disappointment evident. "Adelaide, you must be realistic. The rumors won't die down on their own, and staying here without a husband will only make things worse."

"I know," I replied, tears welling up in my eyes. "But I can't marry a man I don't love, not just to escape the scandal. I can't do that to myself, and I can't do that to him."

My mother sighed, her eyes softening with sympathy. "But what will you do, darling? The longer this goes on, the more difficult it will be for you to find a way out."

"I don't know," I admitted, my voice breaking. "But I can't give up on myself, not yet. There has to be another way."

The room fell silent, the weight of my decision hanging heavily in the air. My father shook his head, his disappointment palpable, but he said nothing more. My mother's eyes were filled with concern, but also with a glimmer of understanding.

As I left the drawing room, the weight of the rumors and the escalating pressure felt like a noose tightening around my neck. But even as I teetered on the edge of despair, I knew that I couldn't let fear dictate my choices. I couldn't marry Mr. Crawford just to escape the scandal.

I had to find another way, a way that didn't involve sacrificing my chance at true happiness. But as the rumors continued to swirl around me, I couldn't help but wonder how much longer I could hold out before the storm finally broke.

33

The Escape Plan

The rumors had grown unbearable. Each day brought new whispers, more vicious and elaborate than the last. The walls of Windermere Manor felt like a prison, and the pressure from my parents to accept Mr. Crawford's proposal weighed on me like a ton of bricks. Though I had refused, the idea of remaining in London—where I was judged and scorned at every turn—was becoming increasingly unbearable. I felt trapped, suffocated by the expectations and the scandal that had engulfed me.

I knew I couldn't stay any longer. The thought of enduring another day under the weight of society's scrutiny, of facing the judgmental stares and the cruel gossip, was too much to bear. My heart ached with the knowledge that my dreams of a future in London, of finding true love, were slipping away. And so, with a heavy heart, I made the decision to leave it all behind.

The plan was simple: I would pack my things and leave in the dead of night, before anyone could stop me. I would travel far away from London, to a place where no one knew my name, where I could start fresh without the burden of my past. It wasn't the life I had envisioned for myself, but it was the only escape I could see.

As I quietly packed my belongings, the weight of my decision settled heavily on my shoulders. I moved through my room, carefully placing the few items I cherished into a small trunk. The rest—gowns, jewels, the trappings of a life I no longer recognized—I would leave behind. There was no room for them in the life I was about to embark on.

But as I prepared to flee, a sense of unease gnawed at me. I couldn't shake the feeling that I was leaving something unfinished, that there was one last thing I needed to confront before I could truly be free. I tried to push the thought away, telling myself that this was the only way forward, that I couldn't afford to look back.

I left the manor and closed the door very quietly. I walked stealthily until I thought none of the servants would hear me. I breathed a sigh of relief when I reached the courtyard. I was startled from my thoughts by a sudden, the sound of approaching footsteps. My heart leaped into my throat as I froze, my breath catching in my chest. No one was supposed to know about my plan.

"Adelaide?"

Bastian?

Panic gripped me as I realized he had somehow found out about my plan to leave. How could he have known? My mind raced, searching for a way to avoid this confrontation, but there was no escape.

Bastian stood before me, his face a mask of concern and determination. His eyes, usually so guarded, were filled with a raw intensity that took my breath away.

"What are you doing here?" I demanded, struggling to keep my voice steady.

"I could ask you the same," he replied, his gaze flicking to the half-packed trunk behind me. "You're planning to leave London, aren't you?"

I turned away, trying to hide the pain that surged within me. "I don't have any other choice. There's nothing left for me here, Bastian. I can't stay."

He stepped closer. "You can't run away, Adelaide. You can't just disappear and hope the world forgets."

"And why not?" I shot back, the frustration and despair bubbling to the surface. "What's left for me here? More rumors? More scandal? You're about to marry Lady Isabella, and I'm the one left with nothing. I'm doing what I have to do to survive. And why does it matter to you? You've made it clear that I'm on my own."

Bastian's expression softened, but there was a flicker of something—regret, perhaps—beneath the surface. "You've got it all wrong, Adelaide. I'm not marrying Lady Isabella. I never had any intention of marrying her."

I blinked, confusion mingling with the turmoil inside me. "But everyone says—"

"They say a lot of things," Bastian interrupted, his voice tinged with frustration. "But they're wrong. Isabella and I—she's nothing more than an old friend. We've known each other since childhood, and she's like a sister to me. There's never been anything romantic between us."

His words left me reeling, the certainty I had clung to crumbling beneath the weight of this new revelation. "Then why did you disappear? Why did you leave me to face this alone?"

Bastian's eyes darkened with emotion. "I thought I was giving you what you wanted—freedom, a chance to find someone you truly loved. I thought that if I stayed away, the rumors would die down, and you would be able to move on without me complicating things further. But I was wrong, Adelaide. I was so wrong."

"Well, you thought wrong," I snapped, the hurt and anger I had been holding back for so long finally spilling over. "All you did was make things worse. Do you have any idea what it's been like for me? The things people have said, the way they've treated me? And you—you just disappeared without a word!"

He took a step closer, his voice pleading. "I was trying to protect you, Adelaide. I thought I was doing what was best for you."

"Protect me?" I echoed bitterly. "You left me to fend for myself while everyone else turned their backs on me. You abandoned me when I needed you most."

The pain in Bastian's eyes was unmistakable as he reached out, his hand hovering just above my arm, as if he was afraid to touch me. "I'm sorry," he said, his voice raw with emotion. "I never wanted to hurt you. I thought that by stepping back, I was giving you a chance to find happiness—real happiness, with someone else."

I shook my head, tears spilling down my cheeks. "Don't you understand, Bastian? I don't want someone else. I—" My voice faltered, the words I had been too afraid to say threatening to spill out.

"Then don't go," he whispered, his voice barely audible. "Stay with me. Let me prove to you that I'm not the man those rumors paint me to be. I don't want to lose you, Adelaide. Not now, not ever."

My heart ached at his words, at the desperation and sincerity in his voice. But the scars of the past were deep, and I couldn't ignore the pain he had caused, the abandonment I had felt.

"Please, Adelaide," He pleaded, his voice cracking with emotion. "Don't go. I made a mistake—a terrible mistake—but I'm here now. I'm not going to leave you again."

"Why now, Bastian? Why did it take you so long to come back?"

"Because I was a fool," He admitted, his voice barely above a whisper. "I thought I was protecting you by staying away, but all I did was leave you vulnerable. I can't change the past, but I can be here now. I can help you fight this, together."

"What if I stay and nothing changes?" I asked, my voice trembling. "What if you leave again? What if the rumors never go away?"

Bastian took my hands in his, his grip gentle but firm. "I won't leave you again, Adelaide. I swear it. I'll face whatever comes with you, and we'll fight this together. Just... don't go. Don't leave me."

For a long moment, I was silent, my heart torn between the desire to trust him and the fear of being hurt again.

"I don't know if I can trust you again."

"I'll earn it back," He vowed, stepping closer until He was only inches away. "Whatever it takes, Adelaide. I won't let you down again."

"Please," He whispered, reaching out to gently take my hand. "Don't go. Stay with me. Let me prove to you that we can make this work."

Finally, I took a deep breath, searching his eyes for the truth. "I'll stay," I said softly, "but only if you keep your word and honest with me, Bastian. No more running, no more leaving me to face things alone."

Bastian's expression softened, relief flooding his features. "I promise," he said, his voice filled with conviction. "No more secrets, no more running. I'll stay by your side, no matter what."

The words hung in the air between us, a fragile truce formed in the wake of our shared pain. There was still so much to say, so much to confront, but for the first time in what felt like forever, I felt a glimmer of hope.

34

The Price of Silence

After my confrontation with Adelaide, my thoughts in turmoil. Seeing her hurt, watching the tears in her eyes as she spoke of her pain and betrayal, had shaken me to my core. For the first time in my life, I had no idea what to do, how to make things right. I had always prided myself on being in control, on knowing exactly how to handle any situation. But with Adelaide, every instinct I had ever relied on seemed to fail me.

I had tried to protect her. I truly believed that by stepping back, by giving her space, I was doing what was best for both of us. When I first realized she wasn't pregnant, my heart had shattered. I had dared to hope that the child we might have had would bind us together, that it would give me the chance to build a future with Adelaide. But when that hope was dashed, I was left with nothing but uncertainty.

Without a baby to tie us together, I feared Adelaide would leave. She had never loved me—not truly—and I knew it. Her heart was still tangled up in dreams of another life, another man. So, I made the difficult decision to give her the freedom I thought she needed. I chose to stay away, to let her find the love and happiness she deserved, even if it meant losing her forever.

But the rumors refused to die down. Instead, they grew louder, more vicious, until they threatened to destroy not only Adelaide's reputation but also everything I held dear. I told myself that I had done the right thing, that Adelaide needed time to move on, but the nagging doubt wouldn't leave me.

I couldn't shake the image of her wounded face, the pain in her eyes as she accused me of abandoning her.

One afternoon, Lady Isabella, my childhood friend and confidante, paid me an unexpected visit. Her presence was a welcome distraction from the turmoil of my thoughts, but I could see the concern in her eyes as soon as she stepped into my study.

"Bastian," she began, her voice tinged with urgency. "I've heard the rumors. They're getting worse, and I think I know where they started."

I looked up from the papers scattered across my desk, my brow furrowing in confusion. "What do you mean?"

Isabella took a seat across from me, her expression grave. "It's a few individuals from the higher circles—people who have never liked you. They've been spreading lies about you and Adelaide, trying to ruin both of you. I confronted one of them yesterday. They're determined to bring you down, Bastian."

My heart sank as I processed her words. So, the rumors were not just idle gossip. They were a calculated attack, designed to hurt me—and, in the process, destroy Adelaide. The realization sent a surge of anger through me, but it was quickly followed by something far more unsettling: guilt. This was my fault. I had thought I was protecting Adelaide, but in my silence, I had allowed these rumors to fester and grow.

"And what about Adelaide?" I asked, my voice thick with concern. "How is she?"

Isabella's eyes softened, a flicker of sympathy crossing her face. "She's struggling, Bastian. The rumors are hurting her more than you know. She feels isolated, abandoned. She doesn't understand why you left her to face this alone."

Guilt clawed at my chest, tightening like a vise around my heart. I had thought that by stepping back, I was giving Adelaide what she needed, but instead, I had left her to face the storm on her own. I had failed her in the worst possible way.

The image of Adelaide's wounded face flashed through my mind again, and I couldn't stand it any longer. Without another word, I rose from my desk, my decision made in an instant.

"Bastian, where are you going?" Isabella called after me, her voice tinged with worry.

"To fix this," I replied, my tone grim. "I can't let this go on any longer."

Without waiting for her response, I strode out of the room, my mind set on only one thing: reaching Adelaide. I couldn't stand the thought of her suffering any longer, not when I had the power to make it right. I saddled my horse, my movements fueled by a sense of urgency I hadn't felt in a long time. The rumors had gone on long enough, and it was time to put an end to them—no matter what it took.

The ride to Windermere Manor was a blur of pounding hooves and racing thoughts. As the familiar landscape rushed past me, my mind churned with everything that had gone wrong. I had tried to give Adelaide space, to let her find her own way, but all I had done was leave her vulnerable to the cruelty of others. I had thought I was protecting her, but in reality, I had only abandoned her when she needed me most.

When I finally arrived at Windermere Manor, my heart sank as I saw the state of the place. The once lively estate now seemed cold and quiet, as if the life had been drained from it. I found her in in the courtyard, just as she was about to leave. The sight of her trunk, the look of resignation on her face—it was more than I could bear.

"Adelaide," I said.

She turned to face me, her eyes widening in surprise and then narrowing in anger. "What are you doing here, Bastian?"

"I could ask you the same," he replied, his gaze flicking to the half-packed trunk behind me. "You're planning to leave London, aren't you?"

Her expression hardened, and she crossed her arms over her chest. "I don't have any other choice. There's nothing left for me here, Bastian. I can't stay."

"You can't run away, Adelaide. You can't just disappear and hope the world forgets."

"And why not?" She shot back. "What's left for me here? More rumors? More scandal? You're about to marry Lady Isabella, and I'm the one left with nothing. I'm doing what I have to do to survive. And why does it matter to you? You've made it clear that I'm on my own."

"You've got it all wrong, Adelaide. I'm not marrying Lady Isabella. I never had any intention of marrying her."

"But everyone says—"

"They say a lot of things," I interrupted, my voice tinged with frustration. "But they're wrong. Isabella and I—she's nothing more than an old friend. We've known each other since childhood, and she's like a sister to me. There's never been anything romantic between us."

"Then why did you disappear? Why did you leave me to face this alone?"

My heart ached at her words, and I took a step closer, desperate to make her understand. "I thought I was giving you what you wanted—freedom, a chance to find someone you truly loved. I thought that if I stayed away, the rumors would die down, and you would be able to move on without me complicating things further. But I was wrong, Adelaide. I was so wrong."

"Well, you thought wrong," She snapped, the hurt and anger she had been holding back for so long finally spilling over. "All you did was make things worse. Do you have any idea what it's been like for me? The things people have said, the way they've treated me? And you—you just disappeared without a word!"

I took a step closer, my voice pleading. "I was trying to protect you, Adelaide. I thought I was doing what was best for you."

"Protect me?" She echoed bitterly. "You left me to fend for myself while everyone else turned their backs on me. You abandoned me when I needed you most."

"I'm sorry," I said. "I never wanted to hurt you. I thought that by stepping back, I was giving you a chance to find happiness—real happiness, with someone else."

She shook her head, tears spilling down her cheeks. "Don't you understand, Bastian? I don't want someone else. I—"

"Then don't go," I whispered, my voice barely audible. "Stay with me. Let me prove to you that I'm not the man those rumors paint me to be. I don't want to lose you, Adelaide. Not now, not ever."

She looked away, her lips trembling as she fought to maintain her composure. "It's too late, Bastian. The damage is done. I can't stay here anymore."

"Please, Adelaide," I pleaded, my voice cracking with emotion. "Don't go. I made a mistake—a terrible mistake—but I'm here now. I'm not going to leave you again."

She turned back to me, her eyes filled with tears. "Why now, Bastian? Why did it take you so long to come back?"

"Because I was a fool," I admitted, my voice barely above a whisper. "I thought I was protecting you by staying away, but all I did was leave you vulnerable. I can't change the past, but I can be here now. I can help you fight this, together."

"What if I stay and nothing changes?" She asked, her voice trembling. "What if you leave again? What if the rumors never go away?"

"I won't leave you again, Adelaide. I swear it. I'll face whatever comes with you, and we'll fight this together. Just... don't go. Don't leave me."

For a long moment, she was silent, her eyes searching mine for the truth. Then, finally, she let out a shaky breath, the anger in her expression softening into something else—something closer to hope.

"I don't know if I can trust you again," she said, her voice trembling.

"I'll earn it back," I vowed, stepping closer until I was only inches away. "Whatever it takes, Adelaide. I won't let you down again."

She hesitated, her gaze flicking to th trunk and then back to me. I could see the conflict in her eyes, the war between her fear and her desire to believe me.

"Please," I whispered, reaching out to gently take her hand in mine. "Don't go. Stay with me. Let me prove to you that we can make this work."

Slowly, she nodded, her fingers tightening around mine. "I'll stay," she said softly, "but only if you keep your word and honest with me, Bastian. No more running, no more leaving me to face things alone."

"I promise," I said, my voice filled with conviction. "No more secrets, no more running. I'll stay by your side, no matter what."

As I looked into Adelaide's eyes, I knew that I had come close to losing her—too close. My heart pounded in my chest as I searched Adelaide's eyes, praying that she could see the sincerity in mine.

Slowly, I reached up and cupped her cheek, my thumb brushing gently across her soft skin. She didn't pull away, but there was a hesitance in her eyes, a wariness that made my heart ache. I knew that I had hurt her deeply, that I had failed her when she needed me most, and I could only hope that she would give me the chance to make it right.

"Adelaide," I whispered, my voice trembling with emotion, "I'm so sorry. For everything."

Her breath hitched, and I saw the tears that she had been holding back begin to spill over. I hated myself for being the cause of her pain, for making her doubt herself, doubt us.

"I was so afraid," she admitted, her voice breaking. "I thought you didn't care. That you had moved on, that I was just... nothing to you."

I shook my head, my heart shattering at her words. "You were never nothing, Adelaide. You were everything. I just—I didn't know how to be what you needed. I thought I was doing the right thing by giving you space, but all I did was leave you alone."

Her gaze softened, and for the first time, I saw a flicker of understanding in her eyes. "I was afraid too," she confessed, her voice barely above a whisper. "Afraid that if I stayed, I'd end up alone. That you'd leave again."

I tightened my grip on her hand, my other hand still resting against her cheek. "I'm here now," I said, my voice filled with determination. "And I'm not going anywhere, Adelaide. I'll be here, every day, every step of the way."

She looked up at me, her eyes glistening with tears, and for a moment, we just stood there, the distance between us closing, not just physically but emotionally. There was a vulnerability in her expression that made my heart swell with both love and regret. I had caused her so much pain, but I was determined to spend the rest of my life making it up to her.

Without thinking, I leaned in, my lips brushing against hers in the lightest of kisses, testing, asking for permission. She didn't pull away—instead, she leaned into the kiss, her fingers gripping the front of my coat as if she was afraid I might slip away.

The kiss was soft at first, tentative, both of us still so unsure, so afraid of breaking the fragile connection we had just rebuilt. But as the moments passed, the kiss deepened, becoming something more—a promise, a plea, and a declaration all at once.

I poured everything I had into that kiss, all the words I hadn't said, all the emotions I had kept locked away. Her lips were warm and soft against mine, and I could feel her heartbeat against my chest, quickening in time with my own.

I slid my hand from her cheek to the back of her neck, pulling her closer, needing to feel her against me, to reassure myself that she was really here, that she hadn't left. She responded in kind, her arms wrapping around my neck as she pressed herself against me, her breath hitching as the kiss grew more urgent, more desperate.

I could taste the salt of her tears on her lips, could feel the tremor in her hands as they clutched at me. It was a kiss filled with longing, with the ache of everything we had lost and the hope of everything we could still have.

When we finally broke apart, we were both breathless, our foreheads resting against each other's as we tried to catch our breath. I kept my arms around her, holding her close, as if afraid that if I let go, she might disappear.

"Adelaide," I murmured, my voice thick with emotion, "I love you. I've loved you from the moment I first realized what a future with you could be. I was a fool not to tell you sooner, not to fight for you when I had the chance. But I'm here now, and I'm not going to lose you again."

She looked up at me, her eyes wide and shining with unshed tears. "Bastian, I—I love you too," she whispered, her voice trembling. "I think I've loved you for longer than I realized. But I was so scared, so unsure... I didn't know how to let myself feel it."

My heart soared at her words, and I couldn't help but smile, a mixture of relief and joy flooding through me. "You don't have to be scared anymore," I promised, brushing a stray lock of hair behind her ear. "We'll face everything together, Adelaide. The rumors, the scandal—none of it matters as long as we have each other."

She nodded, her arms tightening around me as if to hold on to the promise I had just made. "Together," she echoed, her voice full of hope and determination.

I leaned down and kissed her again, this time with all the passion and love I had held back for so long. There was no hesitation, no fear—only the deep, unyielding certainty that this was where we both belonged. In that moment, with her in my arms, I knew that we could weather any storm, face any challenge, as long as we were together.

35

A Choice Made

The warmth of Bastian's embrace lingered long after he had left Windermere Manor that night. His words, his kiss, and the look in his eyes had solidified something deep within me—a truth I had been too afraid to face for so long. I loved him. Despite everything that had happened, despite the pain and the misunderstandings, my heart had always belonged to him. And now, I had to make the hardest decision of my life.

The next morning, I awoke with a sense of clarity that had been absent for weeks. The rumors, the scandal, the expectations of society—they all seemed to fade into the background as I focused on what truly mattered. I had to confront my family, to make them understand that my future was not something that could be decided by convenience or societal pressure. It was time to choose love, to choose Bastian, and to embrace the uncertainty of the path ahead.

As I made my way to the drawing room, where my parents and Anne were already gathered, my heart pounded in my chest. I knew this would not be easy. My father's stern demeanor, my mother's worry, and Anne's quiet concern all weighed heavily on me, but I couldn't turn back now. I had to stand firm in my decision.

When I entered the room, they all looked up, their expressions a mixture of surprise and anticipation. My father, seated in his favorite armchair, set down the newspaper he had been reading, his eyes narrowing as he studied me.

"Adelaide," he began, his voice heavy with expectation, "have you made a decision regarding Mr. Crawford's proposal?"

I took a deep breath, steeling myself for what was to come. "Yes, Father, I have."

The room fell silent, the weight of my words hanging in the air. My mother, seated beside my father, leaned forward, her expression hopeful. "And what have you decided, darling?"

"I'm not going to marry Mr. Crawford," I said, my voice steady but firm. "I've made my choice, and it's not the one you expected."

"Who are you going to marry? No one wants you here since the big scandal?"

"You're right, Father. No one wants me to be his wife but one person. That person would be Duke Bastian."

My father looked shocked. "Are you serious, Adelaide? Duke Bastian of all people in England?"

"Yes, Father."

My father's brow furrowed, and I could see the disappointment in his eyes. "Adelaide, this is not a decision to be taken lightly. Mr. Crawford offers you a respectable future, free from the scandal that has plagued us. Are you certain this is what you want?"

I nodded, meeting his gaze with unwavering resolve. "I am. I've realized that a life of convenience, of respectability, isn't what I want. I need more than that—I need love, passion, and the chance to build a future with someone I truly care about."

My father's expression darkened, and he leaned forward, his voice low and intense. "Adelaide, Bastian is not the right choice for you. He abandoned you when the rumors started, left you to fend for yourself while he hid away. How can you trust him after that?"

I swallowed, the sting of his words cutting deep, but I refused to back down. "He made mistakes, Father. But so did I. We both have regrets, but we've learned from them. I believe in him, and I believe in what we can build together."

My father shook his head, his disappointment evident. "And what makes you think he'll propose to you? What if he leaves you again? What if this 'love' you speak of is nothing more than a passing fancy to him?"

"He won't leave me," I insisted, my voice trembling with the intensity of my emotions. "He's coming here this afternoon—to propose."

The room went utterly still, my words hanging in the air like a challenge. My mother gasped softly, her hand flying to her mouth in surprise. Anne's eyes widened, her expression one of shock and curiosity. But my father—my father's face darkened with a mixture of disbelief and anger.

"Adelaide, this is madness," he said, his voice rising with frustration. "You're letting your emotions cloud your judgment. Bastian Lightwood is not a man who can be trusted with your future. He's proven that already."

I took a step forward, my heart pounding as I met my father's gaze. "I know you're trying to protect me, Father, but this is my decision to make. I'm choosing Bastian, and I'm choosing him because I love him. Not because it's convenient or respectable, but because it's real."

My father rose from his chair, his eyes blazing with anger. "And what happens when he breaks your heart again? What happens when he decides that his reputation is more important than you? Will you come running back to us, expecting us to pick up the pieces?"

Tears welled up in my eyes, but I refused to let them fall. "I don't know what the future holds, Father. But I know that I can't live my life in fear. I can't marry someone I don't love just to avoid the possibility of pain. I have to follow my heart, even if it means taking a risk."

My father's expression softened slightly, but the anger and disappointment remained. "Adelaide, I've always wanted what's best for you. But this—this is not it."

My mother, who had been silent until now, finally spoke, her voice trembling with emotion. "Adelaide, darling, are you sure? Are you sure Bastian is the one for you?"

"I'm sure," I replied, my voice steady despite the turmoil in my heart. "I'm sure because I know what it feels like to live without him. And I don't want to do that anymore."

Anne stepped forward, her eyes filled with sympathy as she placed a hand on my arm. "If this is truly what you want, then I'll support you, Adelaide. But know that it won't be easy. You'll have to fight for this, for him."

"I know," I whispered, tears finally spilling over. "But I'm ready. I'm ready to fight for the man I love."

My father let out a heavy sigh, running a hand through his hair as he looked at me with a mixture of frustration and resignation. "I can't say I approve of this, Adelaide. But if you've made up your mind, then there's nothing more I can do. Just remember, you're choosing a hard path."

"I know," I replied, my voice trembling with emotion. "But it's my path. And I have to walk it."

As the conversation ended, and my family slowly came to terms with my decision, I felt a mixture of relief and trepidation. I had chosen love over convenience, passion over respectability. The road ahead would be uncertain, fraught with challenges and risks, but it was a path I was willing to take— because it was the path that led to Bastian.

And as I waited for him to arrive that afternoon, my heart swelled with anticipation, hope, and the knowledge that I was finally taking control of my own destiny.

36

A Proposal Accepted

T he hours that followed my declaration felt like an eternity. My heart raced with a mixture of hope and dread as I waited for Bastian to arrive. My family, especially my father, remained tense and unspeaking, the air thick with unspoken concerns. I could sense their unease, their doubts about the path I had chosen. But I was resolute; this was my decision, and I would stand by it.

Finally, the sound of carriage wheels crunching on the gravel driveway broke the silence. I could barely breathe as I watched Bastian's sleek black carriage come to a halt outside Windermere Manor. My father's eyes narrowed as he glanced out the window, his posture rigid and unyielding. My mother's hand tightened around her embroidery, her expression one of anxious anticipation. Anne, who had remained my quiet support, gave me a small nod of encouragement as I rose to meet Bastian.

I stepped into the hallway just as the door opened, and there he stood— Duke Bastian Lightwood, the man who had stolen my heart and turned my world upside down. He was dressed impeccably, as always, but there was something different about him today. His usually guarded expression was softened by a mixture of determination and vulnerability. He caught my eye, and I saw the sincerity there, the love that he had kept hidden for so long.

"Miss Blair," Bastian greeted me, his voice steady but tinged with the gravity of the moment. He offered a slight bow before turning to the footman who had accompanied him. The man stepped forward, carrying a small velvet box, which he handed to Bastian with great care.

I barely had time to comprehend what was happening before Bastian took my hand, his gaze never leaving mine. "Adelaide," he began, his voice low and intimate, "there are a thousand things I should have said to you before now. A thousand ways I should have shown you how much you mean to me. But I was a coward, afraid of what loving you would mean. Afraid of how much I needed you."

My breath caught in my throat as I listened to his words, the truth of them cutting through all the doubts and fears that had plagued me. Bastian's fingers tightened around mine, as if he were anchoring himself to me, and in that moment, I felt the depth of his emotions.

"I can't undo the past," he continued, his voice trembling slightly, "but I can promise you that I will spend the rest of my life trying to make up for it. I want you by my side, Adelaide—not because of duty, or convenience, or any of the things that have driven me before. But because I love you. And I can't imagine a future without you."

With that, Bastian slowly lowered himself to one knee, the velvet box in his hand. He opened it to reveal a stunning ring, the center stone a deep blue sapphire surrounded by a halo of diamonds. It was exquisite, but all I could see was the man before me, baring his soul in a way I had never expected.

"Adelaide Blair," Bastian said, his voice filled with emotion, "will you marry me? Will you give me the chance to be the man you deserve, to build a life together that we both long for?"

My heart swelled with love and relief as I gazed down at him. There was no hesitation, no doubt in my mind. This was the man I wanted to spend my life with, the man who had shown me that love could be both terrifying and beautiful.

"Yes," I whispered, my voice trembling with joy. "Yes, Bastian, I will marry you."

A radiant smile spread across Bastian's face as he rose to his feet, gently slipping the ring onto my finger. The weight of the sapphire felt reassuring, a tangible reminder of the promise we had just made to each other. I couldn't stop the tears that welled up in my eyes, nor did I want to. This was the moment I had dreamed of, the moment I had feared would never come—and now it was real.

But even as I reveled in our joy, I could feel the tension in the room, the unspoken questions that hung in the air. Bastian turned to face my father, who had been watching the entire scene with a guarded expression.

"Lord Windermere," Bastian began, his voice firm but respectful, "I know that I am not the man you would have chosen for your daughter. And I understand your concerns, given everything that has happened. But I assure you, sir, my intentions are sincere. I love Adelaide more than words can express, and I am committed to her happiness. I know I have much to prove, and I am willing to do whatever it takes to earn your trust and approval."

My father's eyes remained hard as he studied Bastian, his jaw clenched in thought. "Duke Lightwood," he said, his tone measured, "you speak of love and commitment now, but where were you when my daughter needed you most? Where were you when the rumors began to spread, when she was left to bear the brunt of the scandal alone?"

Bastian's expression tightened, but he met my father's gaze with unwavering resolve. "I was a fool, sir," he admitted, his voice heavy with regret. "I thought I was protecting Adelaide by staying away, by giving her space. But I see now that I was wrong. I should have been by her side, facing the storm with her, not hiding from it. I cannot change my past mistakes, but I am determined to make things right. I will not abandon her again."

My father remained silent for a long moment, his eyes narrowing as he weighed Bastian's words. I could feel the tension in the room, the heavy anticipation as we all waited for his response.

Finally, my father spoke, his voice gruff but tinged with a grudging respect. "You say you love my daughter, Bastian. But love alone is not enough. It must be backed by action, by a commitment to stand by her, to protect her and honor her in all things. Can you promise me that?"

"I can," Bastian replied, his voice steady. "And I do. I will protect Adelaide with everything I have. I will honor her, cherish her, and make her happiness my highest priority. I swear it, on my name, and on my love for her."

My father studied him for another long moment, and I could see the internal struggle playing out in his eyes. Finally, he let out a heavy sigh, his shoulders slumping slightly in resignation. "Very well," he said, his voice reluctant. "I can see that you are sincere, Duke Lightwood. But know this—I will hold you to your word. If you ever hurt my daughter again, you will have me to answer to."

A wave of relief washed over me as my father's stern expression softened slightly, and I knew that, while he might not be fully happy with my choice, he was willing to accept it. My mother, who had been silent throughout the exchange, finally spoke, her voice trembling with emotion.

"Adelaide," she said, her eyes filling with tears, "if this is truly what you want, then we will support you. All we've ever wanted is for you to be happy."

I nodded, my own tears spilling over as I looked at my family—at the people who had stood by me, who had worried and feared for my future, and who were now willing to trust in my choice. "Thank you," I whispered, my voice choked with emotion. "Thank you all."

Anne stepped forward, wrapping me in a warm embrace. "I'm happy for you, Adelaide," she said softly. "Truly. You deserve this."

As Bastian and I stood together, the ring on my finger shining brightly in the light, I felt a deep sense of peace settle over me. The road ahead would not be easy, and I knew there would be challenges to face. But I also knew that I had made the right choice—the choice to follow my heart, to embrace love even in the face of uncertainty.

With my family's support and Bastian by my side, I was ready to face whatever came next. The scandal, the rumors, the whispers of society— they no longer held the power to frighten me. Because I knew that, together, Bastian and I could overcome anything.

And as we prepared to announce our engagement to society, I felt a surge of excitement and anticipation. The scandal that had once threatened to ruin me was now forgotten, overshadowed by the news of the upcoming wedding of the season. It was a new beginning, a fresh start, and I couldn't wait to see what the future would bring.

37

The Wedding

T he weeks leading up to the wedding were a whirlwind of preparations, anticipation, and a flood of emotions that left me breathless.
The scandal that had once threatened to overshadow everything was
now a distant memory, replaced by the excitement surrounding what had
quickly become the most talked-about event of the season. Invitations had
been sent to every corner of high society, and as the day drew closer, I could
feel the weight of it all pressing down on me—but in the most exhilarating
way.

Windermere Manor was transformed into a hive of activity. Servants
hurried about, attending to every detail, while my mother and Anne busied
themselves with last-minute arrangements. The grandeur of the occasion
was almost overwhelming, and yet, amidst the flurry of preparations, there
was an undercurrent of intimacy, a quiet joy that filled my heart every time I
thought about what was to come.

And then, finally, the day arrived.

The morning of the wedding dawned bright and clear, the sky a perfect
canvas of soft blue. Sunlight streamed through the windows as I stood in my
room, gazing at my reflection in the mirror. My wedding gown, a masterpiece
of ivory silk and delicate lace, hugged my figure with an elegance that made
me feel both regal and fragile. The veil, a cascade of gossamer, framed my
face, its edges fluttering softly as I moved.

Anne entered the room, her eyes shining with pride and emotion as she took in the sight of me. "Adelaide," she whispered, her voice thick with tears, "you look beautiful. Absolutely perfect."

I smiled at her reflection in the mirror, my heart swelling with love for my sister, who had been my constant support through everything. "Thank you, Anne. I don't know what I would have done without you."

She moved to stand beside me, her hand gently squeezing mine. "You're going to be so happy, Adelaide. I can see it in your eyes."

I turned to face her, my emotions threatening to spill over as I hugged her tightly. "I hope so, Anne. I truly hope so."

The door opened, and my mother stepped in, her expression one of pure adoration. "Oh, my darling girl," she murmured, tears glistening in her eyes as she took in the sight of me. "You're a vision."

I blushed under her praise, feeling the full weight of the day settle on my shoulders. This was it—the moment I had been waiting for, the moment that would change everything. My mother moved to adjust my veil, her hands trembling slightly as she fussed over the delicate fabric.

"You're about to embark on a new chapter, Adelaide," she said softly, her voice filled with emotion. "I've watched you grow into a strong, beautiful woman, and I know you're going to be an incredible wife. I'm so proud of you."

Tears welled up in my eyes as I looked at her, the love and pride in her gaze nearly overwhelming me. "Thank you, Mother. That means everything to me."

A soft knock at the door interrupted the moment, and my father stepped in, looking every bit the proud patriarch. His eyes softened as they landed on me, and for the first time in weeks, I saw a flicker of peace in his expression.

"Adelaide," he said, his voice a little hoarse, "you look stunning."

"Thank you, Father," I replied, my voice trembling slightly. "I'm so glad you're here."

He walked over to me, his hand resting gently on my shoulder. "I may have had my doubts, but I want you to know that I support you, Adelaide. If Bastian makes you happy, then I'm happy too."

A wave of relief washed over me, and I nodded, unable to speak as tears threatened to spill over. My father offered me his arm, and I took it, feeling the reassuring strength in his grip as we prepared to walk down the aisle together.

The ceremony was held in the grand hall of Windermere Manor, a space that had been transformed into a haven of elegance and beauty. White roses and lush greenery adorned every surface, their fragrance filling the air. Candles flickered softly, casting a warm, golden glow over the assembled guests, who whispered excitedly as they awaited the arrival of the bride.

As the doors to the grand hall swung open, and my father and I began our walk down the aisle, I felt every eye in the room turn to me. The weight of their gazes, their expectations, was almost overwhelming, but then I saw him—Bastian, standing at the altar, his eyes locked on mine.

He looked every bit the duke, his tall, commanding presence softened by the emotion in his gaze. His dark hair was impeccably styled, and his sharp, handsome features were softened by the tenderness in his expression. But it was his eyes, those deep, stormy eyes, that held me captive. In them, I saw everything—love, hope, and a promise of a future we would build together.

As I walked toward him, each step bringing me closer to the man I had chosen, the man I loved, everything else faded away. The whispers, the scandal, the doubts—all of it melted into insignificance as I focused on the one person who mattered most.

When I finally reached the altar, my father placed my hand in Bastian's, his grip firm as he passed me to the man who would soon be my husband. Bastian's fingers closed around mine, his touch warm and reassuring, and in that moment, I knew that I had made the right choice.

The ceremony began, the officiant's voice a steady murmur as he led us through the vows. Bastian's hand never left mine, his grip tightening slightly as he spoke the words that would bind us together.

"I, Bastian Lightwood, take you, Adelaide Blair, to be my wife," he said, his voice strong and clear, filled with the love and determination that had always drawn me to him. "To have and to hold, from this day forward, for better, for worse, for richer, for poorer, in sickness and in health, to love and to cherish, till death do us part."

As I repeated the vows, my voice trembling with emotion, I felt the weight of each word, each promise, sinking into my heart. This was more than just a ceremony, more than just a public declaration of our love. It was the culmination of everything we had been through, the highs and lows, the pain and joy, all leading to this moment.

When the officiant finally pronounced us husband and wife, Bastian turned to me, his eyes shining with love and pride. He lifted my veil, his fingers brushing against my cheek as he leaned in to kiss me. The moment his lips touched mine, the world around us seemed to disappear. The cheers of the guests, the music, the grandeur of the hall—all of it faded into the background as we sealed our vows with a kiss that spoke of promises kept, of a future we would face together.

As we turned to face the assembled guests, hand in hand, I could see the smiles and nods of approval from those who had once doubted us. The scandal was forgotten, replaced by the excitement and joy of the union before them. We had faced the storm, and we had come out stronger for it.

The reception that followed was a blur of laughter, dancing, and well-wishes. The grand hall was alive with the sounds of celebration, the music and conversation blending into a symphony of happiness. Bastian never left my side, his hand always at the small of my back, his presence a constant reassurance. We moved through the crowd together, accepting congratulations and toasts, but all the while, our focus remained on each other.

As the evening wore on, we found a quiet moment to ourselves, slipping out into the gardens that had been the backdrop for so many of our early encounters. The moonlight bathed the landscape in a soft, silvery glow, and the air was filled with the scent of roses.

Bastian turned to me, his expression soft and full of love. "We did it," he murmured, his hand gently caressing my cheek. "We're finally here."

I smiled up at him, my heart full to bursting. "Yes, we are. And I wouldn't change a thing."

He leaned down, capturing my lips in a slow, tender kiss that sent a shiver of warmth through me. When he pulled back, his eyes were filled with a quiet intensity that took my breath away.

"I love you, Adelaide," he whispered, his voice full of emotion. "And I promise you, I will spend the rest of my life proving it to you."

"I love you too, Bastian," I replied, my voice trembling with the depth of my feelings. "And I can't wait to start our life together."

As we stood there, beneath the stars, I felt a sense of peace and contentment that I had never known before. The road ahead might be uncertain, but I knew that with Bastian by my side, we could face anything. We had weathered the storm, and now, together, we would bask in the warmth of the love that had brought us here.

And as we walked hand in hand toward the reception hall, ready to face the world as husband and wife, I knew that this was just the beginning of the greatest adventure of our lives.

38

Bridal Night of Passion

Bastian and I ascended the grand staircase, hand in hand, our footsteps soft against the plush carpet. My heart pounded with every step, a mixture of excitement and nerves making my breath quicken. Though it wasn't our first night together, this felt different—more profound, more meaningful. Tonight, we were husband and wife, bound by the vows we had exchanged before all of society.

We reached the door to the master suite, which had been prepared for us. Bastian paused, turning to look at me with a gentle smile, his eyes reflecting the same anticipation I felt.

"Are you ready, my love?" he asked softly, his voice a soothing balm to my racing heart.

I nodded, a shy smile playing on my lips. "Yes, I am."

With a tender look, Bastian opened the door and guided me inside. The room was bathed in the warm glow of candlelight, the flames flickering softly in the gentle breeze from the open window. The scent of roses lingered in the air, a reminder of the celebration we had just left behind. The bed, draped in luxurious linens, stood at the center of the room, an invitation to the intimacy we were about to share.

As the door closed behind us, a sense of privacy enveloped us, the world outside slipping away. Bastian turned to face me, his eyes full of love and desire. He reached out, gently brushing a stray lock of hair from my face, his fingers lingering on my cheek.

"You are so beautiful, Adelaide," he murmured, his voice husky with emotion. "I've thought about this moment for so long."

I blushed under his gaze, my heart swelling with the warmth of his words. "And I've dreamed of it too, Bastian. But now that it's here, I—"

He silenced me with a soft kiss, his lips gentle against mine. "There's no need to say anything," he whispered, his breath warm against my skin. "Tonight is about us, about being together as husband and wife."

His words calmed the flutter of nerves in my chest, replacing them with a deep sense of trust and love. Bastian's hands moved to the delicate buttons at the back of my gown, his touch sure and steady as he began to undo them. I could feel the tension in the fabric easing with each button he released, the cool air of the room brushing against my skin.

As the gown slipped from my shoulders and pooled at my feet, I stood before him in only my chemise, the thin fabric clinging to my form. Bastian's eyes roamed over me, a look of admiration and desire in his gaze that made me feel both vulnerable and cherished. He stepped closer, his hands trailing down my arms as he leaned in to kiss my neck, his lips leaving a trail of warmth along my skin.

"Adelaide," he murmured against my collarbone, his voice thick with emotion, "I want you to know that I love you—completely, utterly. Tonight is not the night for us, my love. But I want you to think of this bridal night as the one that erases all wounds."

We laughed as we reminisced about our accidental one-night stand that had caused quite the scandal among the upper class. "Tonight, I will put those rumors to rest," Bastian promised, as he traced his fingers down my arm.

"I'm not afraid of getting pregnant now," I replied, with a coy smile. "After all, we are married now."

I reached up to undo the buttons of his waistcoat, my fingers trembling slightly. Bastian stood still, allowing me to undress him, his gaze never leaving mine. There was a tenderness in his eyes that made my heart ache with love for him, a vulnerability that mirrored my own.

Once his waistcoat and shirt were discarded, Bastian drew me into his arms, the warmth of his bare skin against mine sending a thrill through my entire body. He kissed me deeply, his hands sliding down to the small of my back as he pressed me closer to him. The kiss was a promise, a reassurance that tonight would be about us, about the love we shared.

Gently, Bastian guided me toward the bed, his touch careful and respectful. He lifted me onto the soft linens, his eyes dark with desire as he joined me, his body hovering above mine. The intimacy of the moment was overwhelming, but in the best possible way. I could feel the heat of his skin, the strength of his muscles, and the tenderness in his touch.

He took his time, his hands exploring my body with reverence, his lips following the path his fingers traced. There was no rush, no urgency—only the slow, deliberate unfolding of our love. Bastian's touch was both familiar and new, each caress a reminder of the connection we shared, a connection that was now deepened by the vows we had exchanged.

He leaned in to kiss me. Our kiss was hot and passionate, and I could feel the heat rising in my body as his tongue explored my mouth. Bastian climbed on top of me. His fingers traced the curves on my stomach, and I sighed with pleasure as his lips moved down to kiss my lips, my neck, and then my nipples.

I could feel his hardness pressing against me, and I moaned with pleasure as his lips moved down to his stomach. I hoped he would do it soon, and I didn't have to wait much longer.

As he finally settled between my legs, his gaze locked with mine, I felt a rush of emotion—love, trust, and a sense of belonging that I had never known before.

Bastian took out his cock and played with it in mine until he thrust several times, and we both reached release. "Oh, Bastian," I moaned, as he filled me up.

"You like that, don't you?" he asked, as he continued to thrust.

"Yes, Bastian, yes," I replied, as I wrapped my legs around his waist.

Bastian leaned down to kiss me, his lips soft and warm against mine as he slowly entered me, our bodies joining in a way that felt both natural and sacred.

The sensation was exquisite, a mix of pleasure and tenderness that made my breath catch in my throat. Bastian moved with a slow, steady rhythm, his hands cradling my face as he kissed me deeply. There was no need for words; our bodies spoke for us, each movement a testament to the love we shared.

We changed positions several times, trying out different angles and speeds. Bastian took me from behind, and I could feel his balls slapping against my ass as he thrust deeper and harder.

"Fuck, you feel so good," he groaned, as I moaned with pleasure.

"Yes, yes, don't stop," I begged, as I felt another orgasm building up inside me.

The world outside ceased to exist as we lost ourselves in each other, the only sounds the soft sighs and murmurs of our lovemaking. Bastian's touch, his kisses, his whispered words of love—all of it wove together to create a symphony of sensation that enveloped me completely. I had never felt so connected to another person, so completely at peace.

Bastian's fingers found their way to my clit, and he started to rub circles around it. "Come for me, my love," he whispered, as I screamed with pleasure.

I could feel Bastian's cock twitching inside me, and he filled me up with his hot cum. "Oh, fuck," he groaned, as he collapsed on top of me.

When we finally reached the peak of our passion, it was a shared moment of bliss that left us both breathless, our bodies trembling with the intensity of it. Bastian held me close, his arms wrapped around me as we lay together in the aftermath, our hearts beating in time with each other.

As we lay in the quiet of the night, the room bathed in the soft glow of the dying candles, I felt a deep sense of contentment settle over me. This was where I was meant to be, in the arms of the man I loved, the man I had chosen to spend my life with.

We lay there, panting and sweating, as we caught our breath. "I love you, Bastian," I whispered, as I traced my fingers down his back.

Bastian brushed a tender kiss against my forehead, his voice a low murmur in the darkness. "Thank you, Adelaide, for choosing me. For loving me."

I smiled, my heart full to bursting as I snuggled closer to him. "Thank you for being the man I always knew you were, Bastian. I love you, and I always will."

We drifted off to sleep in each other's arms, the world outside forgotten as we lay entwined in the warmth of our love. The scandal, the doubts, the fears—they were all behind us now. What lay ahead was a future filled with promise, with the joy of a love that had been tested and had come out stronger on the other side.

And as I closed my eyes, I knew that this was only the beginning of our journey together, a journey that would be filled with challenges, but also with the kind of love that would see us through anything.

39

Epilogue

The summer sun bathed Lightwood Manor in a golden glow, the warmth of the day reflecting the happiness that had settled into every corner of our lives. The gardens were in full bloom, a riot of color and fragrance, and the soft breeze carried with it the laughter and joy that had become a constant in our days. It had been only a few months since our wedding, but already it felt as though Bastian and I had been together forever—a lifetime of love packed into such a short time.

Life as Bastian's wife had turned out to be everything I had hoped for, and more. The man I had married was no longer the distant, guarded duke who had once hidden his heart behind a mask of cold reserve. Instead, he was warm, affectionate, and utterly devoted to me—and to the little one growing inside me.

I smiled to myself, a wave of contentment washing over me as I placed a hand on my swollen belly. A month after our wedding, I had discovered that I was pregnant, a revelation that had sent ripples of excitement and joy through the household. Of course, rumors had immediately begun to spread— whispers that I had been pregnant before the wedding, that our hasty union had been nothing more than a cover for a scandalous affair. But Bastian and I had shared a private laugh at the absurdity of it all. We knew the truth: our love had blossomed, quite literally, on our wedding night.

Now, as I sat on a cushioned bench in the manor's sun-drenched garden,

I watched the world around me with a serene sense of fulfillment. My hand rested protectively over my belly, which had grown large and round with the life that thrived within. The baby—our baby—was six months along, and the anticipation of meeting our child had filled our hearts with a joy that words could scarcely capture.

I glanced up as Bastian emerged from the manor, his tall figure casting a shadow across the lawn as he made his way toward me. He was as handsome as ever, his features softened by a smile that spoke of contentment and love. When he reached me, he didn't hesitate to gather me into his arms, pulling me onto his lap with a tenderness that never failed to make my heart skip a beat.

"How is my beautiful wife today?" he murmured, pressing a soft kiss to the top of my head as his hand found its way to my belly, rubbing slow circles over the fabric of my dress.

"I'm wonderful," I replied, leaning into him with a sigh of contentment. "And your child seems to be particularly energetic today."

Bastian chuckled, his hand stilling as he pressed his palm flat against my belly, feeling for any signs of movement. "I can't believe it, Adelaide. In just three months, we'll finally meet our little one."

His words sent a thrill of excitement through me, and I smiled up at him, my heart swelling with love for this man who had become my world. "It feels like a dream, doesn't it? Everything we've been through, and now here we are—waiting for our child."

Bastian's expression softened, his eyes shining with a warmth that melted away any lingering shadows of our past. "I remember imagining this," he admitted, his voice low and filled with emotion. "I used to picture you just like this—your belly round with our child, sitting on my lap, content and happy. And now, seeing it come to life... It's more than I could have ever hoped for."

I felt my eyes mist with tears, but they were tears of happiness, of overwhelming love. "I never thought I could be this happy," I whispered, my hand covering his on my belly. "But you've given me everything, Bastian. A love I never knew I needed, a family to call my own."

He smiled, his gaze never leaving mine as he leaned in to capture my lips in a kiss that was both tender and passionate. The world seemed to fall away in that moment, leaving only the two of us, joined by the love we had fought so hard to preserve.

As our lips parted, Bastian rested his forehead against mine, his breath mingling with mine. "I love you, Adelaide. More than I ever thought possible."

"And I love you," I replied, my voice trembling with the intensity of my emotions. "Thank you for choosing me, for standing by me."

Just as we were about to kiss again, a sudden, powerful movement from within my belly caused us both to gasp in surprise. The baby kicked, a strong, determined motion that sent a ripple of laughter through me.

Bastian's eyes widened in delight as he felt the movement beneath his hand. "Did you feel that?" he asked, his voice filled with awe.

"I did," I said, laughing softly as the baby kicked again, as if in response to our joy. "I think our little one is just as excited to meet us as we are to meet them."

Bastian's face lit up with a smile so wide it made my heart ache with love. He leaned down and pressed a kiss to my belly, his voice soft and full of wonder. "We can't wait to meet you, little one. You have no idea how much you're already loved."

The baby kicked again, and I couldn't help but laugh at the delight on Bastian's face. It was a moment of pure happiness, of the kind of joy that comes from knowing you are exactly where you are meant to be, with exactly the right person.

As we sat there, basking in the warmth of the sun and the love that surrounded us, I felt a sense of peace settle over me. We had faced so much, overcome so many obstacles to be together, and now we were on the cusp of a new adventure—one that would bring us even closer.

Bastian looked up at me, his eyes filled with a love that took my breath away. "We've come so far, haven't we?"

"We have," I agreed, my voice soft with emotion. "And I wouldn't change a single thing. Every challenge, every moment of doubt, led us to this. To each other."

He kissed me again, a lingering kiss that promised a future filled with love, laughter, and endless possibilities. "No matter what comes, Adelaide, we'll face it together. As equals, as partners, and as a family."

I smiled against his lips, feeling the baby kick once more, as if agreeing with his father's words. "Together," I echoed, my heart full to bursting. "Always."

And as we sat there, wrapped in each other's arms, our future stretched out before us like a bright, endless horizon. It was a future filled with love, with adventure, and with the promise of a life lived to the fullest.

And I knew, without a doubt, that we were ready to face it—all of it—together.

* * *

You can read Anne Blair and Colin Ashford's story in Marquess's Unexpected Bride.

CRESSIDA BLYTHEWOOD

THE MARQUESS'S UNEXPECTED BRIDE

About the Author

Cressida Blythewood is an author of Regency romance novels, renowned for her warm, heartwarming love stories that transport readers to a time of elegance, wit, and enduring passion. With a deep affection for the Regency era, Cressida weaves tales that celebrate the power of love to overcome societal boundaries, misunderstandings, and personal trials, all while ensuring that her characters find their way to a happy ending.

Also by Cressida Blythewood

Falling for the Rogue's Charm

Chased by a rogue in her dreams, pursued by him in reality—what's a matchmaker to do when love refuses to follow the plan?

Made in the USA
Monee, IL
31 March 2025

14959466R00105